stuck on you

the misadventures of **Willie Plummet**

PAUL BUCHANAN
& ROD RANDALL

CPH®
SAINT LOUIS

The Misadventures of Willie Plummet

Cover illustration by John Ward.
Back cover photo by Ira Lippke.
Cover and interior design by Karol Bergdolt.

Scripture quotations are from the HOLY BIBLE, NEW INTERNATIONAL VERSION®. NIV®. Copyright © 1973, 1978, 1984 by International Bible Society. Used by permission of Zondervan Publishing House. All rights reserved.

Copyright © 1999 Rod Randall
Published by Concordia Publishing House
3558 S. Jefferson Avenue, St. Louis, MO 63118–3968
Manufactured in the United States of America

Library of Congress Cataloging-in-Publication Data

Buchanan, Paul, 1959-
    Stuck on you / Paul Buchanan and Rod Randall.
       p.   cm. — (The misadventures of Willie Plummet : 13)
    Summary: Inspired by mishaps to his remote control model car and his friend Felix's glasses, eighth grader Willie Plummet, a creative genius with a talent for misadventures, tries to come up with a new kind of super glue.
    ISBN 0-570-05567-9
    [1. Inventors Fiction. 2. Christian life Fiction.] I. Randall, Rod. II. Title. III. Series: Buchanan, Paul, 1959- Misadventures of Willie Plummet : 13.
PZ7.687717St 1999
[Fic]—dc21   99–21183

1 2 3 4 5 6 7 8 9 10   08 07 06 05 04 03 02 01 00 99

For Leigh

Contents

The Axle Avenger

My hands oozed with sweat. Keeping a grip on the remote control was getting tougher by the second. My latest creation, the Axle Avenger, sparkled like a ruby in the afternoon sun. The hood was almost as red as my hair. The wire antenna bent with the hot breeze. Mitch stood down the street behind his remote control car, waiting for the cue.

"Don't worry, Willie," Felix said. He patted my back to reassure me. "Mitch's car looks like a little green pom-pom."

"A what?" I glanced at Felix. For some reason, he wasn't wearing his glasses. I was so stressed out I hadn't noticed. "That's no pom-pom. It's a tank."

"Serves you right," Sam said. Her real name was Samantha. When it came to the truth, she told it like it was. "Only a dweeb would get suckered into playing chicken with a model you just finished. I'll bet the glue isn't even dry."

"This wasn't my idea," I reminded her.

We had all been in the cafeteria when Mitch started talking about his new remote control car, the Green Machine. I probably shouldn't have chimed in, but I couldn't help myself. His sister, Megan, was sitting right there. She has big brown eyes and silky brunette hair. For some reason, whenever she's around, I'm desperate to prove myself. The fact that Mitch and I have a history of racing didn't help. We once went head to head at the dump with our remote control cars. My Dumpcruiser 5000 lost big time. We became good friends after that, but I still dreamed of a rematch.

Too bad that wasn't going to happen. Leonard "Crusher" Grubb, the thug of Glenfield Middle School, rode his skateboard to meet us at Mitch's house with a plan of his own. He told everyone that a race was a waste of time. He reasoned that if Mitch won, it wouldn't prove anything. Mitch had already beaten me once. If I won, we'd be tied, which wouldn't prove anything either. He said that playing chicken was the only way to decide once and for all who ruled in remote control cars.

"Unless you don't have the guts for it," Crusher broadcasted while looking at me. Megan was standing right there when he said it.

I looked in her eyes and then back at Crusher. "What are we waiting for?" I had the guts for it, all right. The fact that they were tied in a knot proved it.

I had spent weeks working on the Axle Avenger. I started with an extra large remote control car, then added all kinds of custom details. My family owns Plummet's Hobbies, so coming up with parts was easy. I mounted real headlights, a spoiler, and a miniature license plate that read *Plummet*. I even installed a radio that worked. The Axle Avenger was one cherry machine.

"On your marks!" Crusher shouted for all to hear. "Get set ..."

I took a deep breath. My clothes stuck to my sweaty skin. Adrenaline rushed through my body.

"Go!"

I pushed the remote lever down. The Axle Avenger's wheels spun out. Rubber burned. The Axle Avenger launched across the pavement like a dragster. Mitch's car barreled forward, heading straight for mine. The space between the cars dropped to fifty feet. Forty.

"He's not turning away," Sam warned.

"He will," I assured her. But even as I said it, I could feel my confidence draining like the color from my face.

The Axle Avenger swallowed the pavement in front of it. I hoped the glue was dry by now. I had finished up a few details before coming over. I used the most expensive glue we had in the store, the Rolls Royce of adhesives.

The cars drew together like magnets. Thirty feet. Twenty.

"The way I see it, the cars won't even hit," Felix said to reassure me. He squinted like he was watching two rockets.

"Go find your glasses!" I snapped, getting irritated. My hands shook. I glanced at Mitch. His green machine kept coming. Ten feet to impact. Five.

I almost turned away, but didn't.

Crash!

The Axle Avenger exploded like a stick of plastic dynamite. The frame bounced off of Mitch's car and landed on its side. Parts flew in every direction. The Green Machine held its ground, parked upright and looking fine.

"Awesome!" Crusher shouted. He jogged to the crash sight. Everyone followed.

"Too cool!"

"That ruled!"

Cheering filled the air. With everyone so jazzed over the crash, it almost seemed worth it. Then Crusher reminded me it wasn't.

"Plummet, you got spanked!" he laughed. In an instant, the crowd went from mesmerized to mean.

"Nice work, Willie," someone laughed.

"Really," a kid added. "What'd you make that thing out of?"

"Catch a clue on how to glue," another scoffed.

I didn't have a comeback, so I focused on my car. I righted the frame and tried backing it up. The electrical engine hummed for a moment, then stopped. To make things worse, the radio came on. It sputtered out an oldies tune. I think it was "Yesterday" by the Beatles.

"A working radio?" Crusher said in mock amazement. "That was a nice car."

The crowd formed a circle around both cars. Mitch didn't say anything at first, then he looked at me and shrugged. "We should have just raced."

"Raced?" Crusher gagged. He put his arm on Mitch's shoulder. "Look at Plummet's car. You blew it to bits. You're the champ, Mitch. The champ."

"No way," Felix said, coming to my defense. "Mitch's car looks just as damaged as Willie's."

Everyone stared at the cars for a blank moment, then at Felix. The subsequent explosion of laughter sounded almost as loud as the crash. Crusher moved to the center of the circle and gestured with open hands. "Get your glasses, Patterson. Plummet's car is toast. Parts are everywhere."

I hoped Felix would quiet down. Instead of helping me, he was making things worse. But he moved to the crash sight, determined to prove his unprovable point. "So the Axle Avenger lost a few parts. Big deal." He reached down to pick up the stick shift, but grabbed Crusher's shoe lace instead.

Crusher watched in disbelief as Felix yanked it loose. "Get away from me, Patterson! You're dangerous." He shoved Felix away.

Wobbling backwards, Felix stepped on one of the Axle Avenger's tires. His foot flew out from under him and he was airborne. I cringed at what was coming. Felix landed on what little remained of my car. The music stopped, but the sound of crunching plastic went on.

Pretty soon kids were judging his fall.

"I give him an 8.6," one said.

"More like a 9.9," another added. "He had the height. The distance. Sensational!"

Even Crusher waxed poetic. "His landing was a thing of beauty."

Everyone busted up, and it sounded like we were in the middle of a studio audience. Then Felix let out a moan and rolled over. The blood on his shirt quieted everyone down.

Sam knelt beside him. "Felix, what happened?"

"Something stabbed me in the back," he said through clenched teeth.

Crusher slugged my arm. "What'd you build that piece of junk out of, daggers?"

"Knock it off," I said. "You pushed him."

A sense of dread spread over the crowd. Sam examined the blood stain on Felix's shirt. "Here it is." She pointed to the broken stick shift in his back.

"So just yank it out," Crusher said.

"No!" Sam waved him off. "I need to prop up Felix's head. And I need bandages."

Someone gave Sam a backpack. She used it as a makeshift pillow for Felix. Mitch ran to his house and returned with bandages and antiseptic.

"These will have to do," Sam said. "Everyone stand back."

We obeyed. Sam seemed like she knew what she was doing. Since she volunteered as a candy striper at the county hospital, no one was going to question her. At least at first. Eighth grade guys aren't the most compassionate bunch. The longer it took, the more everyone's patience gave out.

"I'd like to run some tests," Sam said. "If I could get you to the emergency room, I'd recommend an IV. And maybe an MPG."

"MPG?" Crusher questioned. "That stands for miles per gallon."

"I meant EKG," Sam explained.

"Sure you did," Crusher said, mocking her. "What about a VET? We can have Patterson put to sleep, along with Plummet's model."

That got the ball rolling.

"Dr. Sam, should I get some spray paint?" one of Crusher's friends asked. "That way when Felix croaks, we can make an outline of his body in the street."

"Real funny," Sam said.

Felix had a strange look on his face. I couldn't tell if he was holding in laughter or tears. For me, the answer was easy. One look at my car, and I wanted to cry. So much for the Rolls Royce of glues. I might as well have stuck the parts together with my own spit.

Felix continued to moan. After careful examination, Sam decided to remove the broken piece of stick shift. When she did, everyone laughed. It had barely pierced his skin, but that didn't stop Felix from milking Sam's special attention. If it wasn't for the deep rumbling sound headed in our direction, he probably would have stayed in the street all day.

"Car!" I shouted. I knelt to gather up what I could of the Axle Avenger.

"Forget it!" Sam ordered. "Help me with Felix!"

The engine bore down.

For a moment I was paralyzed. My eyes darted between the Axle Avenger, Felix, and the car heading our way.

A Pencil-Splint Geek

Just as I got to Felix, he rose on his own. I grabbed the Axle Avenger and lunged out of the way. A black car roared past. It was one of those classic styles from the 1950s, with a convertible top and lots of chrome. The whitewall tires crunched the parts I had left in the street. The car was easily going double the speed limit.

"Crazy woman driver," I shouted from the curve. The classic car peeled around the corner.

"Are you saying she's a bad driver because she's a woman?" Megan asked. She stood beside me with her arms crossed. Her big brown eyes, suddenly narrow, waited for an answer. From behind her, Sam glared at me, already angry about being teased.

"Um ... no," I stumbled. "That's not what I meant. It's just that ... um ... the driver was driving crazy and happened to be a woman."

"Sure," Megan said. "Whatever you say."

I watched her go inside. Then Sam huffed off without saying another word. My day had just gone from bad to worse. I pulled my shirt up and formed a pouch for the Axle Avenger parts left on the ground.

As Felix and I walked to his house, I learned that Megan and Sam weren't the only ones ticked off at me.

"You would have left me in the street to die," Felix complained.

"I panicked for a second. That's it. Did I try to help or not? Now quit bugging me about it. You're fine, you big wuss." That was harsh, but Felix was getting on my nerves. Since he didn't have his glasses, walking next to him was like playing human bumper cars. "This wouldn't have happened if you were wearing your glasses." We turned up the walk to his house.

"How can I wear them? They're lost."

"Whose fault is that? Why do you take them off so much?"

Felix stopped and grabbed a finger to emphasize each point. "One, they're out of style. Two, the left hinge is broken and held together by a paper clip. Three, they constantly slide down my nose. And four, they make my face sweat, which gives me zits."

"The fourth point is stretching it. We're in the middle of a heat wave. What do you expect?"

"I expect new glasses. But my dad says until I learn to take care of the ones I have, no new glasses."

I stepped onto the front porch. Felix matched me stride for stride, more confident now that he was home. When I grabbed the doorknob, he stopped me.

"Hear that?" Felix asked in a low voice. "My dad's home. If I walk in without my glasses, I'm toast. We'll have to climb in my window." He jumped off the porch, as if my help was no longer necessary.

"Slow down," I whispered.

"What for? I'm home. I know this place like the back of my ..." Konk! A low branch dropped Felix cold. "... hand." After his last accident, I expected Felix to bleed like a river, but he didn't. His thick head came through. Standing up, Felix stumbled in a daze. His confidence was shot along with his sense of direction. He moved like a human pinball. He bounced into the gate, then off a tree. He knocked a pot from the window sill. For a grand finale, he tripped over the hose and hit his knee on a sprinkler. "Ouch!"

"Just stay there," I whispered. I hurried to Felix's side and helped him to the backyard. Somehow, he managed to climb in his window. The tricky part was getting me inside with one hand holding my pouchful of parts. When Felix took the Axle Avenger, I was able to squirm through.

One look at Felix's room, and it was clear why he couldn't find his glasses. It looked like a tornado had touched down somewhere between his bed and clothes hamper.

"They've got to be here somewhere," Felix said in a hushed voice. He quietly closed his door, then started tossing clothes aside.

I helped him search for a few minutes, then gave up. I plopped down on a chair only to hear a distinct cracking sound.

"What was that?" Felix asked.

"It sounded like something breaking, kind of like when you landed on my Axle Avenger."

I stood up and Felix moved the pile of clothes to the floor. There was nothing on the chair. Retrieving the clothes, he shook them one by one. When he got to a T-shirt, out dropped half of his glasses. Next came the other half. The frames had snapped evenly in two at the nose bridge.

"Way to go, Willie. Now I'm really in trouble." Felix fit both pieces together, then pulled them apart.

Footsteps came down the hall, followed by a knock. "Felix, are you in there?" Mr. Patterson asked.

"Yeah, Dad. What's up?" Felix squeezed the two halves together again, then pushed them on his face. Amazingly, they held in place.

Mr. Patterson pushed open the door. "When did you get home?"

Felix stared at his dad, unwilling to move his face or any other part of his body. "A little while ago."

"Really?" Mr. Patterson eyed us both suspiciously. "I didn't hear you come in."

"Weird, huh?" Felix mumbled through tight lips. He could have passed for a ventriloquist.

Mr. Patterson lifted an eyebrow. "Did you come in the front door?"

Felix started to shake his head, then held still. "Not exactly."

"Not exactly," his dad repeated. "What does that mean?"

The suspense was incredible. I watched Felix's glasses as if they were a time bomb. His last move might have finished him. I could see a slight gap where the two halves came together.

"We started to, then came around back instead," Felix explained. To keep his head from moving, he spoke like a robot.

"Then you came in the back door," Mr. Peterson suggested.

"Not exactly," I offered, trying to get Felix off the hook.

"Not exactly, again." Mr. Patterson crossed his arms. "This is getting good."

Felix pressed his finger against his glasses. He tried to be casual, as if all he wanted to do was push the frames up on his nose. But the sides must have come completely apart because he left his finger there. To make things worse, Felix made a weak attempt at changing the subject. "So Dad, how come you're home from work so early?"

"I finished a project ahead of schedule," Mr. Patterson said. "Thought I'd use the extra time to mow the lawn."

"It needs it!" Felix blurted out, as if the lawn was what this was all about.

Mr. Patterson looked at his watch. "I'd better get to it, then." He turned to leave, then paused in the doorway. "However you came in, I'm glad you're home." With that he closed the door. We could hear his steps getting faint as he walked away.

My mouth dropped open. I couldn't believe it. Felix's diversion had worked. It was a miracle. It was a dream. It was a—

The door flew open. Trick.

"GOTCHA!" Mr. Patterson yelled.

I jumped, flinging Axle Avenger parts all over the room. Felix flinched just long enough to let his glasses come apart. He bobbled the halves, but they dropped to the ground.

"Okay, Felix," Mr. Patterson said. "Out with it."

"It's my fault, Mr. Patterson," I stuttered. "I broke Felix's glasses."

"How?"

"I sat on them."

"You sat on them."

I nodded.

"Did you sit on Felix's head?" Mr. Patterson asked.

"No."

"You must have."

"I didn't."

"Then you didn't break his glasses, because Felix doesn't take them off for friends to sit on. He keeps them on. Right, Son?"

I watched Felix for his next evasion. He didn't even try. He explained everything and finished with a renewed plea for new glasses.

His dad wouldn't hear of it. "Take care of the glasses you have, and we'll consider getting new ones. In the meantime, I'd say you have some glasses to mend." Mr. Patterson left, closing the door behind him.

Using my shirt-pouch, I started cleaning up model auto parts. "Looks like we've got some repair work to do. Don't worry—I've got a big idea that will solve both of our problems. Meet me tomorrow after school in the lab."

"I can't wait," Felix said. He pushed his glasses together and put them on. They fell apart as soon as he let go.

Normally, hanging out in the back room of Plummet's Hobbies is a blast. We call it "the lab" and use it as our headquarters for conducting cool experiments.

With the air conditioner broken, though, the store felt like a sauna, even with the doors and windows open. With Glenfield in the middle of a heat wave, we were burning up.

"Can't we do this somewhere else?" Felix complained.

"I thought of that. But everything we need is here." I surveyed the materials spread over the table. "Felix, if everything comes together, my creative genius will reach new heights."

"Or new lows," Sam cut in, as she entered the room, shaking her head.

"Who invited her?" I asked, looking at Felix. "With friends like that, who needs enemies?"

"I'm sorry, Willie." Sam lifted a tube of glue from the lab table, glanced at the ingredients, then put it down. "I'm just stressed out over being a candy striper. I feel like the head nurse is out to get me. Everything I do is wrong. There's just too much to learn."

"Learn?" I laughed. "How hard is it to bring sick people candy?"

"What?" Sam objected. "You have no clue what I do. I have to transport patients in wheelchairs, run errands for the nurses, deliver meal trays. Sometimes I even have to feed patients. And you should see the head nurse. She watches me like a hawk."

Felix ignored Sam's explanation and pretended to be a candy striper. "Sorry about your ulcer, Mr. Burns. How about some Red Hots to cheer you up?"

Sam slugged Felix in the arm. "So that's the thanks I get for fixing your glasses?"

When Felix's repair job fell apart during first period, he had begged Sam for help. Using white medical tape from her backpack and a pencil for a splint, she had fastened the frames together as if she were setting a broken bone.

"Your repair job made me the laughing stock of the school," Felix said. "Crusher called me a 'pencil-splint geek.'"

Sam crossed her forearms on the table, then dropped her head on top of them. Her blond hair hid her face. "Great. Now I'm a failure at the hospital and at school."

"You're not a failure," I said. "Felix is joking. Don't take it so hard. You're all stressed out."

Sam lifted her face. It looked like she might cry. "Physical rehab isn't the easiest ward to be assigned to, you know. Patients are trying to recover from serious injuries or strokes, but it takes time. The things they used to take for granted are difficult for them now, like brushing their teeth or walking. They get frustrated and grouchy. Guess who they take it out on?"

"Don't tell me," I answered. "You?"

"Exactly. To make things worse, there's this weird orderly that gives me the creeps. Supposedly he was hit by lightning. Now he's got a screw loose or something."

Felix scratched his head. "You're freaked out by an orderly?"

"That's right," Sam admitted. "Gordy the orderly."

"Gordy the orderly?" I laughed and turned to Felix. "Try saying that three times fast."

Felix went for it. "Gordy the odory ... Gordily orery ... Gorery or ... forget it!"

"What'd I tell you?"

Sam crossed her arms. "You guys are worse than they are."

"Lighten up," Felix told her. "There must be some nice people there."

"A few," Sam admitted. She thought for a moment. "There's a man named Mr. Meridian. He's really nice. But just watching him makes me sad. He told me that before his stroke, he played golf all the time. Now he needs a walker just to hold himself up. He takes slow tiny steps, then needs to rest. He's lonely and bored."

"Doesn't his family visit him?" Felix asked.

"Supposedly his daughter came a few times. Now she's away on business."

Suddenly, I felt guilty for teasing Sam. I tried to come up with something that would help. "What about watching TV or reading?"

"I go around with the magazine cart all the time. They're tired of it. They want to do something else."

I looked at the destroyed Axle Avenger and got an idea. "What about model building? It involves doing something. They'd love it!"

"Could work," Sam said, mulling it over. Then she shook her head. "No way. The head nurse would never buy it. She'd come up with some reason to say no. I'd feel dumb for even suggesting it."

"No you wouldn't," Felix said. "It's a good idea."

"It's a great idea," I said, congratulating myself.

Sam stood up and paced. "Maybe it's worth a try. I'll bring it up on my next shift."

"Get some samples from my dad to take with you," I suggested. "He might even offer a discount and free delivery."

"That would help," Sam admitted. She headed to the front of the store to talk to my dad.

I returned my attention to the bottles and tubes on the lab table. My goal was to create the world's strongest model glue, one that would bond on contact and hold like steel. No more waiting and waiting for glue to dry. My plan involved mixing adhesives until I came up with the ultimate combination. I'd call it the StuckTight 2000. And best of all, I'd use only nontoxic brands, so I wouldn't have to worry about breathing dangerous fumes.

Before Felix and Sam arrived, I had gathered every glue, epoxy, and plastic cement that I could from the store. We sold several varieties, and we had a bunch more that companies sent us as samples. Next, I numbered each one with a black felt marker. Felix's responsibility was to keep accurate records as I mixed the different brands.

"Let's start with numbers one, two, and three," I said.

Felix picked up number one. "It says, 'Keep away from children.' You'd better stand back."

"Real funny." I unscrewed the caps and placed a drop from each sample on a square piece of paper. I expected Felix to start writing, but he was distracted. He crossed his eyes to stare at the medical tape that held his glasses together. Next, he rolled his eyes to get a look at the pencil splint that ran along the top of the frames.

"Felix! Pay attention!"

"Calm down, Dr. Crankenstein," he snapped. "You try concentrating with a pencil taped to your head."

"It's taped to the frames, not your head."

"Close enough."

I exhaled in disbelief. "I can't believe you haven't changed that splint yet."

"No way," Felix told me. "I've got a plan. One look at these frames, and my parents will agree to buy me new ones. Even they won't want me looking this stupid." Felix nodded with conviction, feeling proud of himself.

"You're the man, Felix. Now can we get started?"

Felix spoke as he wrote. "One drop of number one, one drop of number two, and one drop of number three. Got it." He leaned over and marked #1 on the square piece of paper.

Removing a toothpick from the box, I stirred for a while, then held it straight up in the glue mixture for ten seconds. When I let go, the toothpick remained upright for a moment, then slowly dropped to the table.

"Not a bad start," Felix said. He made a few notes about mixture number one.

"I'll take it. But we can do better." My plan was to keep trying until we came up with a formula that would hold the toothpick in an upright position. I figured it was just a matter of trial and error. Unfortunately, after covering the lab table with dozens of combinations, I was beginning to think it would be all trials and nothing but error. At first the glues didn't dry fast enough. Then we added catalyst, and they dried too fast.

Things were looking pretty bad when Orville, my older brother, rushed through the back door. He worked in the store in the afternoons and evenings. A gust of hot air followed him and suddenly the glue-covered sheets of paper began to move. "Orville! Close the door."

"Forget it," he shot back. "It's like an oven in here."

"Close it!" I ordered. "Close it!" I encircled the test papers with my arms, hoping to keep them in place. But it was no use. The hot wind lifted the papers from the table. I stumbled backwards, but not in time. The toothpicks came at me like poison darts.

Pillow Problems

"Yikes!" I yelled. "Ouch! Ouch!"

First, the toothpicks poked my skin, then the papers held tight. It was like I had been tarred and feathered. Orville doubled over, laughing.

"Oh sure, laugh at me when it's your fault," I grumbled, pulling at the glue samples. They clung like leeches to my face and shirt. The ones that stuck to my arm hairs hurt the worst.

Sam returned before I finished. "Now that's commitment. Actually testing your new product on yourself. By the way, Willie, you missed one."

"I'll get it," Orville said. He grabbed a paper square next to my ear. Instead of just pulling it off, he smeared it across my face.

"Yeow!" I wailed and jerked away.

Orville stared at the paper square in his hand. "Number thirteen? That's your age, Willie. What a funny coincidence."

"Real funny," I grumbled.

After hearing us argue for a while, Sam stepped in. "What I want to know is, did you come up with the dream glue or not?"

I returned the last of the samples to the table. "Or not. This afternoon has been a big waste of time."

"No?" Orville cried in mock amazement. He headed for the front of the store. "My little brother, waste time? It can't be!"

"No offense, Willie," Sam offered, "but you can't expect to invent the world's greatest glue just by mixing other glues. Why is it so important to you, anyway?"

"What?" I gagged. "My family owns a hobby store. I should have the fastest and strongest models in town! You saw what happened to my Axle Avenger. I need a glue that bonds on contact and holds like steel."

"What's wrong with waiting for glue to dry?" Sam questioned. "Maybe an instant bonding glue wouldn't be such a good thing. I think what you need is patience."

I mimicked her with a baby voice. "I think what you need is patience."

"Make fun if you want," Sam persisted. "But you know I'm right. Patience is a fruit of the Spirit. There's a Bible verse that talks about it. Check it out."

"It's Galatians 5:22–23," Felix put in. "Sam's right. You need patience, like me. Look how long I've waited to get new glasses."

"Yeah—and complained every step of the way," I reminded him. "You have less patience than I do." I turned to Sam. "Fruit of the Spirit, huh? What about joy? That's in there too. You're so stressed out over being a candy striper, you don't know what joy is."

From there, the argument only got worse. At times, it was two on one. At times, we were all against each other. We didn't stop until my dad came into the lab carrying several boxes of models.

"Sorry to interrupt your fun," he said, his voice full of sarcasm. "Start with these, Sam. They'll give the head nurse a good idea of what's available. If it's a go, Willie will gladly deliver what you need."

"What?" I protested. Using an old rag, I worked at the glue on my face. "Listen, I've done the delivery thing, and it's no picnic. Remember my custom invention, the Sidewalk Dogsled? That thing was a handful. Besides, I haven't even developed a world-class glue yet."

"Maybe not, but your makeup looks world-class," Sam teased. "That shade really brings out the highlights in your hair."

I made my way to the bathroom mirror and cringed. The rag I'd used had red paint on it. My cheeks looked like they were covered with blush. Everyone enjoyed a laugh on me. That improved their attitudes in a hurry, but not mine. Sam's remark about the fruit of the Spirit really got to me. Maybe I wasn't the most patient kid on earth, but what was wrong with wanting to invent a great glue?

"Later, gorgeous," Sam called to me as she headed out the back door. "I'm due at the hospital by five. I'll let you know when we need our first delivery."

"Sure," I grumbled. I turned on the faucet and splashed water on my face. After pumping out a handful of liquid soap, I started to scrub.

"Is it coming off?" Felix asked. He stood in the doorway next to me. "'Cause if it doesn't, maybe you should invent a world-class soap instead."

"Real funny," I mumbled, trying to keep the soap out of my mouth.

Felix slapped me on the back. "Well, I'm outta here. My parents should be home by now. I want them to see my frames. One look and it's new glasses for me."

Water dripped from my face into the sink. After drying off, I checked the mirror. Lint from the towel stuck in patches where the glue had touched my skin, but at least the paint was gone. I stood there feeling sorry for myself. Sam had a plan to improve her standing at the hospital. Felix had a plan to get new glasses. But I was no better off than when I started.

At least, that's what I thought then. The next morning I found out otherwise ... big time.

"Willie, get up!" my mom yelled from downstairs. "Breakfast is ready."

I opened my eyes, but didn't move. My pillow clung to my face. I tried to lift my head, but my pillow wouldn't let go. At first I thought it was a dream. Then I realized it was a nightmare. I tugged at the pillow-case, but it held fast to my face. If I pulled any harder, my skin would come with it.

I sat up in bed and crossed my arms. My pillow sat up with me, stuck tight. The weight pulled at my skin and hurt. I held it with my arm. That's when Orville walked by my room.

"You heard Mom," he told me. "Quit hugging your pillow and get out of bed."

"Tell Mom I'll be down in a few minutes. I need to ... um ... wake up more or something." I held my pillow to my face as I spoke. If Orville found out what had happened, I'd never hear the end of it.

"You'll walk to school if you're not ready."

"Fine," I said, still not moving.

Orville took note and decided he knew my problem. "Ah, does little Willie have a toothy-achy? Poor baby."

"No, I don't have a toothache. Just tell Mom I'll be there in a few minutes." I laid back down to conceal the fact that my face hadn't left the pillow.

"Mom!" Orville called out, unwilling to let up. "Something's wrong with Willie."

Moments later my mom came to my room, followed by my dad and older sister Amanda.

"He's faking it," Amanda told my parents. "He probably forgot to do his homework."

"No, I didn't," I argued.

"It's something with his face," Orville explained. "He's been clutching that pillow like a security blanket."

My mom stood next to my bed. "Willie, what's wrong?"

I hesitated. I could fake a toothache, stomachache, or headache. I had ache options galore. But sooner or later, they would find out the truth, and I'd feel guilty for lying. I decided to fill them in.

"I sort of glued my pillow to my face," I said sheepishly. I sat up and let go. My pillow didn't.

An eerie silence swept over the room. My family stared at the pillow, then exchanged glances with each other. So much for silence. My room went from library-quiet to laugh-track loud in a split second.

"Ah-ha-ha-ha!" Orville bellowed.

My mom snorted she was laughing so hard. My dad's eyes watered. Amanda held her sides and gasped for air.

"You guys have to promise you won't tell anyone," I begged.

"Oh sure," Orville taunted. He opened my window. "Attention Glenfield! You'll love this one: Willie Plummet glued his pillow to his face!"

"Looks like that pillow is stuck on you," Amanda said.

"'Stuck on You?'" Mom questioned. "That's my favorite Lionel Richie song."

"A sticky situation indeed," Dad added.

"Laugh all you want," I said. "But I'm not going to school until I get this thing off."

"Why not?" Orville said in amazement. "When class gets boring, you can use your pillow to take a nappy-pooh."

"You'll start a new trend at Glenfield Middle School," Amanda said. "Pretty soon, everyone will come to school with pillows glued to their faces."

"All right, that's enough," Dad said, coming to my defense. He removed the pillow from the pillowcase so there wouldn't be as much weight on my face. "If we don't hurry, we'll all be late. Willie, come with me to the garage. I'll find something to get that off."

I followed my dad, but Amanda stopped me. She swirled the pillowcase on top of my head. "Now if it doesn't come loose, you can wear it as a turban. When you get to a closed door, just say, 'Open Sesame.' "

"Cool hat," Orville teased, giving me an exaggerated thumbs up. "That looks awesome, Dude."

If I could have glued pillows in their mouths, I would have. I made my way to the garage as fast as my feet would take me. Even without the pillow inside, the weight of the pillowcase was beginning to hurt my skin.

"This should do the trick," my dad said. He dipped a cotton ball in some paint thinner. "How'd this happen anyway?"

I told him everything.

"You should have cleaned up with something stronger than hand soap," he reasoned. He dabbed paint thinner where the pillowcase was stuck to my skin. After a few seconds, he tugged. The pillowcase didn't budge. He dabbed some more on my cheek. I winced, feeling him pull a little harder.

"Hmm, that's strange," he mumbled. "Let's try something else." He soaked the cotton ball in turpentine and drenched the glue with it. He repeated the process until turpentine ran down my neck; the glue wouldn't give. "Willie, I don't know what you invented, but this glue is incredible. I'll have to try my Super Solvent."

"Your Super Solvent?"

"That's right. I invented it years ago." He grabbed a clean cotton ball and opened a bottle of strong smelling stuff. It felt cool and tingly against my cheek. After letting it soak for a few seconds, my dad tugged on the pillowcase. It worked. "Go wash your face."

I hurried to the bathroom. Using Amanda's face cleanser and plenty of water, I washed up. Except for the long red mark on my cheek, my face was fine. At the breakfast table, Amanda and Orville started another round of wisecracks, but this time I didn't care. All I could think about was what my dad had said, "This glue is incredible."

Somehow, I had come up with a world-class glue after all. Number thirteen would be the StuckTight 2000. All I needed were Felix's notes so I could make a batch. I wolfed down my pancakes and headed upstairs. I got dressed, brushed my teeth, and gathered up my homework in record time. I had to get to school and find Felix. But just as I stepped outside, Orville drove away.

The StuckTight 2000

By the time I got to school I was late, so Felix was already in class. I searched for him between first and second periods, but he never came to his locker. The weird thing was that everyone else had seen him and his goofy pencil-splint glasses.

Good thing for me we had Mrs. McNelly's drama class together. We sat next to each other near the back of the class.

"Where have you been?" I asked. I slid my backpack under my desk.

"Making the rounds," Felix said. He took off his glasses and held them up to the light. He breathed on the lenses and rubbed them with his shirt. Each movement was exaggerated, as if to make sure everyone noticed what he was doing.

"Check it out," I said, pointing to the red mark on my cheek. "Number thirteen is it: the StuckTight 2000!

It's incredible." I explained what happened when I woke up.

"You glued your pillow to your face!" Felix bellowed. His laughter filled the room. He sounded more like a hyena than my best friend. With everyone looking at us, Felix took off his glasses, wiped the lenses some more, then put them back on. "I can't believe you glued your pillow to your face!"

Everyone noticed the red streak on my face and joined in the teasing.

"Smart move."

"What a genius!"

When Mrs. McNelly cleared her throat and glared in our direction, Felix squinted at the chalkboard, like all he really cared about was copying down the homework assignment. "Mrs. McNelly, what does that say?"

Mrs. McNelly read the homework assignment to us. "What happened to your glasses?"

Felix explained that I had broken them and that his parents refused to buy him new ones. He would have to make do with the splint, even though his frames didn't fit. That made it harder for him to concentrate. As Felix moaned on and on, I realized that laughing at me and telling the whole class what happened with the glue was just a ploy. What he really wanted was an audience for his sob story.

"Thanks a lot," I said when Mrs. McNelly turned to write on the board. "You set me up just to get attention for yourself."

Felix tried to weasel out of it. "What are you talking about? You glued your pillow to your face. That's funny."

When I just glared at him, Felix exhaled and sunk down in his seat. "Okay, maybe I overdid it. But I'm running out of ideas. My parents just laughed at Sam's pencil splint. My dad really went off. 'Those are one-of-a-kind frames, Son. I'd hang on to those. One day they might be worth something.'"

"That sounds like your dad," I said. "What now?"

"I've got a new plan. I'm going to shame my parents into getting me new glasses. By the time this day is over, the whole town will be talking about my pathetic broken glasses."

I almost said something about learning patience, but after yesterday's argument in the lab, I decided to change the subject. "Listen, I've got to see your notes on number thirteen. If we can figure out exactly how we made it, we can make a fortune. You'll be able to buy a different pair of glasses for each day of the week. Where'd you leave the notes?"

"In the lab, I think," Felix said.

"What do you mean, you think?"

"When we quit, my notes seemed as worthless as your glues. I can't remember if I left them on the lab table or threw them in the trash."

I thought for a moment. It was Wednesday. The trash was picked up this morning. "Why me?" I moaned. "Why me?"

Just as Mrs. McNelly began to recite something, Sam hurried into class. She sat down in front of me.

"Nice of you to join us, Samantha," Mrs. McNelly said. "I thought you were absent." She walked back to her desk and opened the attendance book. Her pencil didn't have an eraser, so she started to search for one.

"Got ya covered, Mrs. McNelly," Crusher announced. He grabbed Felix by the arm and pulled him to the front. "Take care of it, Patterson." When Felix hesitated, Crusher turned Felix's head and lowered him to the attendance book. With the eraser from the splint in the right spot, Crusher moved Felix's head back and forth.

"Thank you, gentlemen. That was very resourceful," Mrs. McNelly said approvingly.

"Don't mention it," Crusher said.

Felix returned to his desk on loose legs.

"Impressive, Felix," I said when he sat down. "Maybe your dad was right about those frames."

Felix rubbed his temples. "I think I have a headache."

"Take two aspirin and call me in the morning," Sam told him.

"Why were you so late?" I asked her.

"I was helping the school nurse," Sam began. Her expression turned dark. "Megan Reynolds came in and—"

"What's wrong with her?" I interrupted, leaning forward.

Sam looked away. "It was her heart. We tried to save her but ..." Sam sniffed and wiped her eyes. "Her final words were, 'Tell Willie I love him.'"

I swallowed hard. "Are you serious?"

"No, you lovesick dope," Sam laughed. "I can't believe you fell for it."

"I knew you were kidding." I glared at Felix so he wouldn't kick into broadcast mode.

"Actually, Megan really did get hurt," Sam told me. "She sprained her pinky trying to catch a football. It slipped through her hands. I helped the nurse fix her up."

I gave Felix an exaggerated wink, ready to turn the tables on Sam. "What'd you prescribe? Snickers or Milky Way?"

"Not that again," Sam complained.

"Why not Butterfinger?" Felix said. "That would have made more sense."

I nodded. "Good one."

"Keep it up, Willie, and I'll take my business elsewhere," Sam shot back.

"What's that supposed to mean?" I asked.

Sam turned around and faced the front, ready to give her attention to Mrs. McNelly. "Meet me at Plummet's Hobbies after school today, and you'll find out."

I had a feeling I knew what Sam was up to, but I didn't care. All the way to the store, I had StuckTight 2000 on the brain. Felix wanted to talk to the principal and a few more teachers before coming over. The fact that Crusher used his head as a human eraser really added to his sob story. He figured his parents would *have* to buy him new glasses just to save face, but something told me that trying to outfox his parents by making them look bad was a big mistake.

As soon as I walked in the back door of the lab, I felt the heat. The air conditioner was still broken. Even worse, the trash cans were empty. If Felix tossed out his notes, we were back to the drawing board. Several of the paper squares were scattered across the lab table, but no notes. I checked under the table, on the floor, and even in the bathroom. No sign of them.

When Felix finally arrived, I laid into him. "Where have you been? I can't find your notes."

"Take it easy," Felix said. "I had to make a few public appearances on the way over. It's just a matter of time until my parents crack."

"Sure, whatever you say. Now let's find the notes."

"The notes?" Felix looked on the lab table, then around the room. When he took off his glasses, I got nervous.

"You threw them out, didn't you?"

He put the end of his glasses on his lip as if he were a professor fielding a question. "It seems like ..." Felix put his glasses back on and did a slow 360. "Ah-ha!"

"What?" I asked, following his eyes.

Felix walked over and grabbed the notepad from a shelf near the bathroom door. "I put it here when you were cleaning off your makeup."

"Real funny," I said. "Just give me the ingredients for formula thirteen so we can make another batch."

"Let's see," Felix said. He pushed his glasses further up his nose. "One drop of number three; two drops of number six; and four drops of number nine."

I assembled the right bottles.

"I wouldn't get too excited if I were you," Felix told me. "According to my notes, formula number thirteen was one of our worst ones. The toothpick fell over as soon as we let go. When we checked it later, the glue was still wet."

I pointed to the red mark on my face. "See this? Once this glue dries, it never lets go."

"So?" Felix questioned. "Lots of glues never let go if you give them all night to dry. I thought you wanted a glue that bonds on contact?"

That threw me. "Um ... I did. But—"

"And another thing," Felix went on. "You want a glue that bonds with plastic and metal, not skin. There are already glues on the market that bond with skin."

I glared at Felix. "You're just full of good news, aren't you?"

"Aren't you glad I kept notes?" Felix asked tongue-in-cheek.

"Not any more." I decided to make another batch of number thirteen just in case Felix mixed up our test samples. This time I used a plastic toothpick and a scrap of metal. After mixing for a few seconds I let go. The toothpick dropped like a one-legged horse.

"Yep. That's a world-class glue all right," Felix teased. "Bonds on contact and holds like steel."

"You're just mad because your parents won't buy you new glasses. I'll bet you even gave me the wrong formula for number thirteen." I grabbed the notepad from Felix.

He gave me a smug look. "Satisfied?"

"Not yet, but I will be." Using Felix's notes, I came across the formulas that dried quickly. By incorporating some of their ingredients, I could modify number thirteen to dry faster. Felix thought it was worth a try, so we got started. The key was the hot glue gun. After a while we had a mixture that held the toothpick straight up as soon as I quit stirring.

"Now what?" Felix asked.

"Time to rebuild the Axle Avenger. Green Machine, kiss your bumper goodbye." We made a batch of our new winning formula and got to work. I dabbed a little glue on the Axle Avenger's steering wheel and held it in place for a few seconds. When I let go, Felix and I watched closely. The steering wheel didn't budge. I tapped it with my finger. The steering wheel held.

"Yes!" I shouted, jumping around. "We did it! No more waiting for glue to dry. No more broken parts. The StuckTight 2000 has arrived. Bring on the Green Machine."

"I wouldn't be so sure," Felix said. "What if the StuckTight 2000 gets brittle when it hardens? I wouldn't ask for a rematch yet. Try it on lots of models. Put it through the ringer."

"That could take weeks," I objected.

"Not if you can get some help."

"Sure. Where am I supposed to find a bunch of people who have nothing better to do than test my glue on their models?"

Just then Sam entered the lab. "Are you ready for my news? Has the suspense killed you?"

"Not even close," I replied.

Sam ignored me. "The head nurse didn't like your model idea at first. But when she asked a few patients, they loved it!"

"That's nice," I said, trying to sound interested.

"You should have seen Mr. Meridian's eyes light up. He's the one I told you about who had a stroke. He bought one of the models on the spot. He stared at the box like it was a long-lost treasure."

"What kind of car was it?" Felix asked.

"I don't know. One from the '50s, I think," Sam replied. She pulled her blond hair behind her ears. "It was kind of strange. When I asked Mr. Meridian about it, he just said it was a family thing. I could tell he didn't want to talk about it."

"That makes two of us," I told her, growing impatient. "Felix and I have work to do."

"You got that right." Sam handed me a list of her first order. "I need four car models and three ship models. Bring them to the physical rehab unit at 7 this evening. Don't be late. Promptness is rule number six in the candy striper handbook."

"So what?" I replied. "I'm not a candy striper."

"Keep wearing makeup and you will be," Felix joked.

"It was paint. And you keep out of this," I told him. I glanced at the list of models. I figured we had most of them in stock, but didn't want to go look for them. All I could think about was my StuckTight 2000.

Then Sam said something that got the wheels in my mind turning. "And one more thing. Make sure you bring glue; lots of it."

I picked up the bottle of StuckTight 2000. "Lots of glue, huh? Any particular brand?"

"How should I know?" Sam said. "Just make sure it works."

"All of our glues work." I drew my eyebrows together in deep thought. "You probably want something nontoxic so the patients won't have to worry about breathing dangerous fumes. Am I right?"

"Sounds good," Sam agreed.

"And probably a fast-drying glue. That way patients with limited coordination won't have to hold the parts for so long."

"Definitely," Sam said with a nod.

"And one that's not too expensive."

"That's for sure. You can keep that Rolls Royce of glues to yourself."

"Don't worry," I assured her. "The glue I have in mind works ten times better. And best of all, it's free."

Sam eyed me with suspicion. "Is this what I think it is? You want my patients to be guinea pigs for your homemade glue, don't you?"

"Well, maybe. But—"

Sam shook her head. "They're in the hospital. Don't you think they have enough problems?"

"Don't worry," I said. "The StuckTight 2000 will make things better, not worse. It's proven. And best of all, it's free." When Sam just looked at me, I knew I had an uphill battle on my hands. But after a ton of persuading, she finally agreed to let me bring it along.

"If they don't want it, offer them a name brand glue instead," Sam said.

"No problem," I told her. "But I'm sure that once they try it, they'll be stuck on it."

"Or it will be stuck on them," Felix added.

"That's what worries me," Sam said.

I started to lift my hand to the red mark on my cheek, but stopped myself just in time.

That evening Orville dropped Felix and me off at the county hospital. He told us to call him as soon as we were finished with the deliveries. I carried the models and sample bottles of StuckTight 2000 in a big sack. Felix walked beside me, adjusting his glasses.

"I still don't think this is a good idea," I told him.

"Trust me. After tonight, I guarantee my parents will buy me new glasses. This hospital was my dad's crowning achievement as an engineer. Everybody here knows him. One look at my glasses, and they'll know me too—and my tragic story."

"Since when is being irresponsible tragic?"

"Whose side are you on?" Felix shot back. As soon as the glass doors parted, he stepped to the information booth and explained who he was. The woman took notice and said she was glad to meet him. From there, Felix moved on to the administrative offices. Most people had already gone home, but some were still working. Felix went from employee to employee like a politician running for office. Each time he told his glasses story, he stretched the truth a little more.

When someone said the vice president was still in his office, Felix could barely contain himself. Neither could I, but for different reasons. On the way there, I let him have it. "Felix, knock it off. Your dad never said he couldn't afford to buy you new glasses."

"Maybe not exactly," Felix defended himself, "but one time he told me he didn't have money to buy me a new pair of glasses every time I lost the old ones."

"He was making a point," I argued. "This isn't about money and you know it."

Just then we arrived at the vice president's office. He wore a neat white shirt and red tie. His gold-rimmed glasses sparkled. He greeted Felix with a handshake. "Someone said you were on the way up here. How's your dad these days?"

"Fine," Felix said. He adjusted his glasses in slow motion. "I wish I was."

"What have we got here?" the vice president asked. "May I?"

Felix gladly handed over the pencil splint glasses. While the vice president looked them over, Felix spun his biggest yarn yet.

"Seems kind of dangerous having a sharp pencil so close to your eyes," the vice president observed. "Very dangerous."

"A friend of mine fixed them for me. Her name's Samantha Stewart. She's a candy striper for this hospital."

The vice president tightened his eyebrows. "Really?"

Felix nodded and looked down. He spoke with soft humility. "I've been asking for new frames, but money's tight around our house. I'm just glad to have a pair of glasses I can call my own."

Good thing we were in a hospital; I was getting sick just listening to Felix. I checked his cheeks, certain I'd find a trail of tears. Forget about a new pair of glasses; he deserved an Academy Award.

I cleared my throat in Felix's direction. "Well, we've got a lot of deliveries to make. We should get going."

The vice president gave the glasses back to Felix. "I'm concerned about the safety of these frames,

Felix. Frankly, they seem dangerous. Perhaps the hospital can help in some way."

I grabbed Felix by the arm. "I'm sure everything will work out. Besides, Felix's custom frames have been a big hit at school."

"Sure they have," Felix complained. He twisted away from my grip and started to explain what Crusher did with the eraser and the attendance book.

That was all I could take. I left Felix with the vice president and headed for the elevator. If I stayed with Felix any longer, I'd be using the StuckTight 2000 on his lips.

I found Sam at the nurses' station on the third floor. "Special delivery."

"It's about time you got here," Sam said in a huff. She led me to the physical rehab unit and handed me a list of who ordered what. "Remember, they're not the most friendly people to be around. Some of them are in pain. Others just want to go home. If they get on your nerves, just be patient with them."

"Get on my nerves? After what Felix just put me through, I can take anything." I gave her the rundown. "Right now he's probably convincing the vice president that his family is living in the dumpster behind the hospital."

"Felix w-wore his pencil-splint g-glasses here?" Sam sputtered. Her face looked as red as the stripes on her uniform.

"You got it. That pencil splint was the best thing that ever happened to Felix. But don't worry. He gave credit where credit was due. He told everyone you made it."

Sam's face went from red to white. "Me?"

I nodded. "And by the way, the vice president wasn't impressed. The word dangerous came up a few times."

Sam wobbled at the knees. She leaned against the wall for support. "This isn't happening. Tell me this isn't happening."

"Sorry," I said. "Felix will be up here soon. You can ask him yourself."

"If he comes anywhere near me, I'll strangle him."

"In that case, it's a good thing we're in a hospital. By the way, I skipped dessert to hurry over here. How about a Milky Way for an old friend?"

Sam squeezed her hands around my throat. "I don't have to wait for Felix, if you know what I mean."

I nodded, my eyes bulging. Sam let go and stormed down the hall in the direction of the elevator. Glancing at the list she had given me, I tried to get my bearings. I wandered the halls for a few minutes, then found the person at the top of the list. I knocked on the door and waited.

"It ain't locked," a gruff voice replied.

I entered with caution. A elderly man wearing a blue robe and slippers sat in a chair next to his bed.

He had a hooked nose and thin white eyebrows. He stared at the wall.

"Mr. Higgins?" I asked.

"Last time I checked." He still refused to look at me.

I introduced myself. "Here's the Model T Ford you ordered."

When Mr. Higgins wouldn't take the box, I placed it on the tray next to him.

"I also have a free sample of glue for you. It's an excellent new product. I was hoping to get your feedback on it." I placed the bottle of StuckTight 2000 next to the model.

"In other words, you're looking for a guinea pig." He grabbed the bottle of glue and opened the top. One look inside and he scowled. "That's not much of a sample."

"Well, it's ... um, really strong stuff. You don't—"

"If it's so excellent, who cares what I think?"

I shrugged. "I was just hoping—"

Someone bumped me from behind. It was Felix without his glasses. I introduced him to Mr. Higgins, but Mr. Higgins ignored him. He was staring at the parts in the model box.

"This isn't the right one!" Mr. Higgins growled. "The picture on the box shows a black truck."

"It was painted," I told him.

"The box doesn't say anything about needing paint."

"Yes it does," Felix offered. "Right on the back." He tried to point out the spot, but without his glasses he didn't know where his hand was going. He knocked over the open bottle of StuckTight 2000.

"Felix," I gasped.

We both dropped to the ground. In trying to grab the bottle, Felix spun it like a top. Glue oozed out. Felix got it all over his hands. By the time I got the lid back on, half of it was gone.

"What a scam," Mr. Higgins complained. "I get half a bottle of cheap homemade glue and no paint."

I replaced the bottle with a full one. Fortunately, I had brought extras. "I'm sure you'll like this glue. Have fun making the Model T." As soon as he paid for the model, I hurried from the room. I took Felix with me and let him have it in the hall. "Way to go, Champ!"

"Me? You should talk to Sam. Before I got up here, things were going great. The vice president said he'd try and get me new glasses. As soon as I stepped off the elevator though, Sam came at me like a tiger. She took my glasses and wouldn't give them back."

"That's what you get for trying to make everyone look bad except yourself." I moved away from Felix. "Now stay here until I finish the deliveries. I'll get you when I'm done."

Felix stood there wiping his hands on his shorts. Something told me that leaving him there was even more dangerous than bringing him along.

It was.

GO WiLLie!

The rest of the deliveries went fine. The people were happy to get their models and try the StuckTight 2000. The fact that it was free really helped. As I left each room, I glanced at the waiting area to make sure Felix was still there. Sometimes he was sitting, other times standing, but he stayed put until I was done—at least almost. With one delivery to go, I checked again. Felix was gone.

All I had left was a jar of red paint for Mr. Meridian. I wanted to finish the delivery and then look for Felix, but I couldn't risk it. What if he wandered into an operating room and bumped a surgeon? Some poor soul might lose a liver. I hurried down the hall. Felix was nowhere in sight. I went to the nurses' station. Again, no Felix. I searched around for Sam, thinking she might help me. I couldn't find her, either.

After a while a nurse noticed my clueless plight. "Can I help you?"

"I'm looking for my friend." I explained to her what Felix looked like.

She thought for a moment. "I saw someone like you're describing in a wheel chair. He was in another wing, but headed toward the waiting area on this floor."

I chuckled to play along. "That's a good one."

She gave me a curious look. "I wasn't joking. Apparently the boy I saw isn't who you're looking for."

"Apparently not," I agreed. But the way things were going, it could have been Felix. I hurried back to the waiting area. Sure enough, the nurse was right. Felix sat in a wheelchair holding a bag of ice to his eye.

"Felix, what happened?"

"All I wanted was a quick drink of water, that's it." He clutched the arm of the wheelchair with one hand and the bag of ice with the other. "But as I felt my way down the hall, I bumped my head on an open door. To make things worse, an orderly saw the whole thing. From the way I was stumbling along, he thought I was a patient in physical rehab."

"Why didn't you tell him the truth?"

"I tried. I told him about Sam fixing my glasses, then taking them. I told him who my dad was, and that the hospital vice president was a personal friend. The orderly just nodded with a look that said, 'Sure, Sonny, whatever you say.'"

I couldn't help but laugh. "Poor Felix. When you tell a lie, everyone believes you. When you tell the truth, no one does."

"You're as bad as Sam. When she saw me in this thing, she went nuts. She still won't give me my glasses."

"Where is she?" I asked.

"I think she went to check on your deliveries. She told me to stay put."

"Stay put, huh? Those words sound familiar to me. I wonder why." I rubbed my chin, hamming it up. "Oh, I remember. You were supposed to stay put earlier, but you couldn't wait for me to get back. No way. That would take patience. And even though you mentioned Galatians 5:22–23 to me, you had to have water right away."

"Sure, rub it in," Felix moaned. He removed the bag of ice for a minute. His eye was puffy and bruised.

"Five minutes," I told him. "Just stay here for five more minutes. Let me make my last delivery, then I'll get you out of here. With or without your glasses."

Felix agreed to wait for me. I headed for Mr. Meridian's room with the jar of red paint. When he didn't answer my knock, I poked my head inside. An elderly man with a bald head and covers pulled up to his chin slept soundly. I tiptoed in to make the delivery. The model he bought from Sam was a '59 T-Bird. The parts were evenly spread out on a table next to him, along with a nail file. He had used it to sand

down the rough edges on each part. I put the paint
and StuckTight 2000 on the table. The money for the
paint was there, along with a notepad and pen. I
wrote out my request that he try the glue, then hurried back to Felix.

Sam was with him, giving him an earful. "If the
head nurse finds out you're my friend and that you
impersonated a patient, do you know what she will do
to me? I'm not even allowed to have visitors!" Sam
shoved Felix's glasses back on his face. The pencil
splint was gone. "There, good as new. Now get out of
that wheelchair before we all get in trouble."

"You fixed my glasses?" Felix gasped. "Why? The
pencil splint was my key to getting new ones."

"Too bad. You heard the vice president. That
splint was unsafe." Sam looked at me. "I borrowed
some of your StuckTight 2000 from one of the
patients. It had better work."

"Oh, it will," I assured her.

Sam grabbed Felix by the collar and lifted. "Hurry
up! Get going!"

Felix tried to stand but couldn't. "I think we have
a problem."

"Like what?" Sam asked.

"My hand is stuck to the icebag. And that's not all
... I'm stuck to the wheelchair too."

"W-What?" Sam choked.

Just then we heard heavy footsteps marching in our direction. A woman with a harsh voice criticized the man with her.

"That's the head nurse," Sam warned.

"And the orderly," Felix added. "I recognize his voice. Now what, Dr. Sam?"

Sam listened for a moment. "I should have known. That's Gordy the orderly."

"*The* Gordy the orderly?" I asked in mock amazement. "Try saying that three times fast."

Felix went for it. "Gordy—dee—odorly. Goy-dee—lee—"

Sam slapped her hand over Felix's mouth. "Don't start that again. Willie, your models were supposed to improve my standing with the nurse, not destroy it." She pushed Felix into a laundry room. I followed. We hid behind the partially closed door.

"Why are you yelling at me?" I whispered. "Felix is the one who got us into this mess."

Before Felix could object, Sam shushed us both. I joined her in peeking into the hallway. The head nurse led the way, stomping in our direction like a drill sergeant. Her skin was as white as her uniform. Her broad shoulders would intimidate a linebacker. Gordy trailed her. He had frizzy brown hair and bubble eyes that looked in two directions. His flat feet slapped the floor. When they paused in front of the laundry room, we held perfectly still. Sam looked petrified.

Gordy looked up and down the hall. "He's got to be here somewhere."

"If someone's playing games on my floor, I want to know about it," the head nurse demanded. "I've got enough trouble keeping tabs on those candy stripers."

Sam's face dropped as if a warrant had just been issued for her arrest. I glanced at Felix. He was still trying to get his hand free from the ice pack. I didn't blame him, but his timing was a little off. He squeezed the ice bag between his knees and yanked. His hand jerked free and flew into his face. On any other occurrence, Sam and I would have laughed our heads off; but under the circumstances, we cringed.

The head nurse heard the slap. So did Gordy. But as they turned toward the laundry room door, a louder and more distressing sound came from across the hall. It was from Mr. Higgins' room.

"Ahhh!" his surly voice let out. A thud followed.

The head nurse and orderly turned around and rushed into Mr. Higgins' room.

"That's our cue," I said. I pulled Felix from the laundry room and we hurried away. One look in Mr. Higgins' room, and we knew what had happened. His slippers were glued to the floor where Felix had spilled the StuckTight 2000. Mr. Higgins was flat as a pancake. The head nurse and Gordy were kneeling on both sides of him. They were so concerned about Mr. Higgins, they didn't notice us. I rushed Felix down the hall toward the elevator. Sam lagged behind, obviously not sure if she should help us escape or help with Mr. Higgins. When another nurse hurried to Mr. Higgins' room, that answered Sam's question. She stuck with us.

Good thing she did.

"Sam, you've got to call Orville—and fast," I said. "Tell him to bring my dad's Super Solvent when he comes to pick us up. Otherwise, the wheelchair is coming with us."

"Can't you just get loose?" Sam asked Felix. "Yank harder—like you did with the ice pack."

"I've been trying," Felix said. "I can't."

"The ice pack was cold and wet from the condensation. But not the wheelchair," I explained. "It's not coming off without solvent."

"If no one is in the break room, I can call from there. You guys wait in here." Sam pushed us into a small janitor's closet. We waited in silence, staring at mops and jugs of industrial cleanser until she returned.

"Done," Sam told us. She grabbed the handles on the back of Felix's wheelchair. "When Orville *finally* got done laughing, he said he would bring the Super Solvent. He should be on his way. Now let's get out of here."

"I can take Felix down," I said, trying to get the handles back.

Sam wouldn't let me. "If I'm pushing him, it will look more like an official checkout."

"You check people out?" I asked. "I thought you just brought them candy."

Sam had flames in her eyes. I decided my timing on that joke wasn't the best.

When the elevator opened, the three of us rushed inside. I hit the *close door* button. When the steel doors slid shut, we all breathed a sigh of relief. It didn't last long. As soon as Sam hit the button for the lobby, Felix freaked out.

"We can't go down there! I introduced myself to everyone when we got here—and I was walking."

"Why me?" Sam asked.

"They'll also notice my glasses are fixed," Felix said.

"No they won't," I told him. I gave him the brown bag that I used for the delivery. "Put this over your head."

"Oh sure," Sam said sarcastically. "That won't attract attention. Just a routine discharge—a patient with a big brown bag over his head."

"Then hold it in front of your face," I said, getting angry. "Act like you're reading the fine print."

They reluctantly agreed to give it a try. When the doors opened, Sam pushed Felix into the hall and toward the lobby. It looked like our plan might work. Not too many employees were around. Then we glanced toward the front doors. The vice president was standing there talking to someone. I skidded to a halt. It was Felix's dad.

I grabbed the wheelchair and did an about-face. I had no idea where I was going, but I decided to get there in a hurry. "Where to, Sam?"

"The cafeteria," Sam said, catching up. "We'll stall there. Go left at the next hall."

I made the turn and picked up my speed. The coast was clear.

Not for long.

Gordy the orderly appeared from a side hall. He pushed Mr. Higgins in a wheelchair. They turned in our direction and came at us full speed.

"Not him," Sam cringed. "Turn around! Turn around!"

"We can't!" Felix said, still hidden behind the bag.

"Then don't let Gordy see you," Sam said. "Willie, move fast and stay out of Gordy's way."

That was impossible. When I picked up the pace, so did Gordy. When I moved to the right, Gordy did too. When I moved left, Gordy followed.

"Felix, we're about to see how stuck to this wheelchair you really are," I warned him. "This is what you call chicken, round two."

"Are you crazy?" he asked.

"Otherwise, we face your dad. Hmm. I wonder what the vice president said to your dad to bring him down here so quickly?"

"I'm toast," Felix admitted.

"You got it," I said. "But if we crash, maybe your glasses will break along with every other bone in your body."

"Gordy wouldn't hit me, would he?"

Sam jogged to keep up. "Remember what I said about a screw loose. I'd lift my feet if I were you."

Felix pulled his knees to his chin. "Mr. Higgins will tell him to stop."

Wrong again.

"That's the kid with the glue," Mr. Higgins snapped. "Get him!"

"Willie, you better turn around," Sam warned.

"Yeah," Felix added.

"No way," I told them, now jogging. But as we got closer, I started to think Sam and Felix were right. Gordy traced my every move. His wild eyes were electric. He plowed ahead.

I edged to the left. Gordy followed. Ten feet to impact. Three. Two. One ...

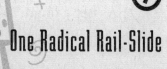

"Now!" Mr. Higgins yelled.

Gordy swerved to the right, just missing us.

Mr. Higgins laughed as they went by. "Did you see their faces?"

"I saw them," Gordy replied. "I saw them."

Seconds later we passed through the cafeteria doors. That's when I realized what had just happened. "I won! Yes!"

"What do you mean you won?" Felix complained. "You practically killed me."

Good thing Felix was in a wheelchair. Otherwise he might have gone for my throat. To make it up to him, I bought him a Snickers and hot chocolate.

"Now what?" I asked Sam.

"There are side exits," she replied, "but we'll look suspicious leaving through one of those. Everyone checks out through the lobby."

"Suspicious?" I asked. "Everything we do is suspicious."

"He's got a point," Felix said.

Sam just shook her head. "I'm fired. Definitely fired."

At school the next day, Mitch and Megan wanted the complete story about what happened in the hospital. I gave them the play-by-play in the ten minutes before first period. "The side exit worked. When Orville showed up with the Super Solvent, we freed Felix from the wheelchair. Sam took it back to the physical rehab unit, along with some Super Solvent. Felix and I got out of there."

"I bet Sam caught it from the head nurse," Megan said. She smoothed her hair to the side. It felt like I was staring, so I forced myself to look away. That's when I noticed Sam coming over.

"The head nurse practically fired me on the spot," Sam explained. "She blamed me for everything, even Mr. Higgins' fall."

"Was he okay?" I asked.

"He was fine. Not only that, he refused to part with the bottle of StuckTight 2000, even when the head nurse asked for it."

"Cool!" I said. "It works!"

"I'm impressed," Megan said. She smiled at me and kept her eyes on mine.

My stomach tightened. I didn't just feel like the world's greatest inventor. I felt like the world's greatest good-looking inventor.

Then Crusher arrived on his skateboard. Like always, he took over. "Check out this rail-slide," he told us. After backing up, he pushed hard to gain speed. He headed for the stairs in front of the school. Once he neared the top of the handrail, he ollied by jumping and bringing the skateboard with him. He landed the skateboard on the handrail and slid down the length of it. Somehow he kept his balance and landed the skateboard on the sidewalk. None of us could believe it.

"Awesome!" Megan said.

I looked at Megan, no longer feeling like the world's greatest good-looking anything. Even Sam clapped for Crusher, which I'm sure was just to get back at me.

Crusher picked up his skateboard and jogged up the stairs. "I can do that all day."

"That was a cool move," Mitch said.

"You try it, Dude," Crusher said. "Go for it."

Mitch shook his head. "No way, I'd probably tweak your board."

"Don't worry about it," Crusher said. He extended the skateboard.

Mitch took the skateboard and looked at the rail. "Sure. I'll go for it."

Crusher gave him a high five. Mitch only had one foot on the board when Crusher stopped him. He noticed me watching. "What about you, Plummet? Are you in?"

"Um ..." I glanced at Megan, whose eyes had returned to me. I was no pro on a skateboard, but I could hold my own. And after my success with the StuckTight 2000, I was feeling larger than life. So what if I hadn't actually done a rail-slide before? There's a first time for everything. This was my chance to outdo Mitch. When I reglued the Axle Avenger, I'd outdo him again. "Sure. Why not? I'm in."

"All right, Mitch," Crusher told him. "Looks like Plummet hasn't learned his lesson."

Mitch pushed the board toward the handrail. He took long strides like a sprinter. At ten feet from the rail, he positioned both feet on the skateboard. At the last second, he crouched down and jumped, bringing the board with him. But he didn't have the height. The skateboard collided with the end of the rail. Mitch flew to the side and tumbled down the stairs.

"Wipeout!" Crusher howled. "Cool!"

Sam ran over to Mitch right away. He struggled to his knees, then his feet with her help. He took a moment to get his bearings. With Sam beside him, Mitch climbed the stairs, grabbing the skateboard on the way.

"Tough break, Dude," Crusher told Mitch, taking the skateboard from him. "This is your chance, Plummet. Make it or break it."

"Break what?" I asked, speaking my mind.

"*Break a leg* is a common expression," a familiar voice said. Felix strolled up next to Sam.

"Don't sweat it, Willie," Sam told me. "If you break a leg, I've got your splint right here." She held up a pencil.

"It worked for me," Felix said. "Well, almost."

With all eyes on me, I put the skateboard on the ground and pushed it back and forth. This was my chance to prove myself, not just to Megan, but to the whole school. The bell would ring in two minutes. Nearly everyone was watching. I looked at the rail, then at my foot.

"Somebody give me a countdown," I said.

"On your mark, get set, go!" Mitch announced.

I kicked the skateboard full speed ahead. My left foot stroked the concrete, pulling it by. My right foot kept balance. I zeroed in on the handrail. Crusher's board seemed stiffer than mine, but it would have to do. The key was making a good ollie. I bent my knee and leaned forward. Another ten feet to the rail. Five feet.

I placed my feet on each end of the skateboard. I squatted, then sprung into the air. The board followed. It felt like I was doing sixty. Maybe I would clear the rail entirely. Maybe I would set a record.

Maybe not.

I had *too much* height. The middle of the skate-board landed hard on the bend in the rail. With my feet on each end, the board snapped in two. If I had-n't lunged to the side, the rail would have sliced me in half. As it was, I landed on my shoulder and tumbled down the stairs.

After how Sam reacted to Mitch's fall, I expected to see her hovering over me as soon as I opened my eyes. All I got was Crusher. He had already gathered up both pieces of his skateboard.

"You're toast, Plummet!" Crusher threatened. He looked at the splintered pieces like they were his heart.

"Toast?" I gasped, scrambling for an excuse. "It's not my fault that—"

"You snapped my skateboard!" Crusher interrupt-ed. "Thanks to your rail flop, it's ruined."

"No, it's not," I told him. The StuckTight 2000 came to mind. "I'll fix it. Your skateboard will be stronger than new."

"He's right," Felix said.

"How?" Crusher asked, not wanting to believe us. He didn't wait for an answer. Instead, he threatened us both. He got so worked up, he was spraying more than he was saying. When he finished, he shoved both of the broken pieces in my arms and stormed off.

Mitch was about to come over when Crusher caught him. The sound of the first bell settled the issue. Crusher and Mitch headed into the building. Megan followed.

Sam came over shaking her head with each step. I rubbed my shoulder, thinking she would offer some emergency care. Guess again.

"Here's that splint I promised." Sam tossed me her pencil, then walked away.

Pretty soon Felix and I were the only ones left outside. I stuck both halves of the skateboard together. Felix untucked his shirt to wipe Crusher's spit off of his glasses.

"Wouldn't it be easier to take off your glasses?" I asked.

"Yep," he answered. "But I can't."

I looked at Felix. "What do you mean you can't?"

"I can't."

"You mean you won't because your dad said not to. After last night, you probably got grounded for a month."

"I got in trouble all right, but that's not what I'm talking about." Felix bent over completely. He held his hands at his side and shook his head. His glasses didn't budge. "Remember what Sam used to glue my frames?"

"You don't mean that—"

"Yep. That's exactly what I mean. Thanks to the StuckTight 2000, my glasses are glued to my head."

Felix, Sam, and I hurried to Plummet's Hobbies as soon as school got out. I put Crusher's skateboard on the lab table in front of me. I grabbed a towel to wipe the sweat from my forehead. It was hot enough on the way over, but thanks to the broken air conditioner, it was even hotter inside. My clothes felt like they had just come out of the dryer.

"I'm ready when you are," I told Felix.

"Any time," Felix answered. He looked at his notes and handed me glue bottles as needed.

I mixed up another batch of StuckTight 2000. In the process I noticed steam on the inside of Felix's glasses. "Are you sure you want your glasses stuck to your nose? A few drops of Super Solvent is all it takes."

Felix shook his head. "No way. My parents want me to keep my glasses on, so that's what I'm going to do. I'll wear these babies 24-7 until they crack."

"Your parents or your glasses?" Sam asked.

"Both!" Felix said with conviction.

Once the StuckTight 2000 was ready, I grabbed both halves of Crusher's board.

"Don't you think you should wait and hear how well the StuckTight 2000 works before you use it on Crusher's board?" Sam asked. "What if the glue doesn't hold and Crusher gets hurt? He'll end up in the hospital, and I'll have to take care of him."

"Crusher in the hospital?" I laughed. "Not in a million years. His bones are too thick to break. He's built like an ape."

"Willie, I'm no Crusher fan, but that's a little harsh," Sam told me.

"But he is an ape. His knuckles have scabs from dragging on the ground."

Sam crossed her arms. "I don't believe you. What were those Bible verses again? Oh yeah, Galatians 5:22–23. I think *kindness* is one of the fruits mentioned. But you wouldn't know about that."

"*But you wouldn't know about that,*" I mimicked. "Maybe kindness is a fruit of the Spirit. But Crusher suckered me into not one, but two, challenges. Both of which ended in disaster. You expect me to show him kindness? Crusher?"

Sam offered a smug expression. "If you had *self-control,* another fruit of the Spirit, you would have said no to those challenges."

Sam had a point, but I didn't have time to dwell on that now. I had a skateboard to fix. "Enough talk. It's glue time."

"You're serious?" Sam asked.

"Sam, you saw how well the StuckTight 2000 worked on Mr. Higgins' slippers. He wasn't going anywhere."

"Neither was I," Felix said. "That wheelchair had me good."

"Exactly," I agreed. "Sam, you apply the Stuck-Tight 2000. I'll squeeze both halves together."

"No way," she said. "I'm out of this."

"I'll do it," Felix offered. He wiped his glasses with a towel. But with the heat, the inside of the lenses still looked foggy.

"Can you see well enough?" I asked.

"Sure." Felix used a strip of wood to smear the StuckTight 2000 on both sides of the broken board. He applied it thick. Too thick.

I squeezed the halves together and held them. Glue oozed up from the crack. "You better clean that up."

Felix grabbed a towel and wiped off the excess. After a few minutes I let go. The bond held. Just to play it safe, I used a bar clamp to press both sides together for fifteen minutes. When I took it off, we could barely see where the skateboard had snapped in two. But the real test would be when I stood on the deck.

I put my feet on the deck of Crusher's skateboard. It held like new. "Yes! The StuckTight 2000 rules! Time to take this bad boy back to Crusher. Who wants to go?"

Sam and Felix just looked at me.

"I have to go alone?" I asked. "What happened to kindness?"

That worked. Sam and Felix reluctantly joined me. Outside, I rode the skateboard while they walked. I offered Sam a ride, but she thought Crusher's board would break. She didn't want to be responsible. Felix took a short turn, but with his cloudy glasses, he didn't last long. That was fine with me. Considering the heat, it was nice to ride instead of walk, especially since Felix let me hold onto his shoulder. I didn't have to push myself. I just stood there and let him pull me along. He said he knew a short cut to Crusher's house, so I enjoyed the ride.

Before long, we were at the top of a sloped street. Looking down the sidewalk reminded me of a ski jump from the Olympics. At the bottom of the hill the street made a sharp turn to the right, which meant that the sidewalk did too. I could never make the turn. But if I crossed the street, I could use the parking lot on the other side to slow down.

"This has potential," I said. "Sam, would you jog ahead and tell me when the street's clear? I want to enjoy this."

Sam raised an eyebrow. "Jog? In this heat?"

"It would be *kind* of you," I said with a grin. I eyed Felix for support.

He nodded back. "Sure would."

"Don't overdo it," Sam warned. She started walking. "I'll wave you on when it's clear."

Once Sam reached the bottom of the grade she held up a flat palm telling me to wait. Good thing she did. A semi came around the corner and climbed the hill in our direction. Sam started to lower her hand then raised it again. This time a classic car squealed into view and sped toward us. Something about it looked familiar.

"Felix!" I blurted out. "That's the car that almost turned you into roadkill."

"Are you sure?"

I thought I was. This time though, there was a man behind the wheel. Patches of grey primer covered the black body. The car powered up the hill.

Something else about it looked familiar. I studied the details: classic convertible, low profile, wide tires, lots of chrome.

"Of course!" I blurted out. "That's a '59 T-Bird! That's the model Mr. Meridian is building." The black car sped past. I turned to watch it go. I tried to step from the skateboard to get a better look. But the skateboard wouldn't let go of my foot. The StuckTight 2000 had done it again.

"There's your signal," Felix said. He pulled his foot away and gave me a push. "It's go time!"

I whipped my head around. The first thing I noticed was Sam's frantic gesture. She flattened her palms in my direction.

"Go time?" I gagged. "It's stop time! Stop!"

Thanks to his foggy glasses, Felix had misread Sam's signal. But he took his mistake in stride. "Dude, relax. Just step off the skateboard."

"I can't!" I shouted. "I'm glued to the deck!" Buildings flew past me in a blur. The sidewalk dropped in front of me like a launch ramp. Only fifty feet to the street! Forty!

Felix chased me at first, then gave up. Sam held her ground until she realized there was nothing she could do. She leapt out of the way. Cars barreled along in both directions. Twenty more feet to the street. Ten. A cement truck rumbled around the bend. Five.

I spotted my only option: the traffic light on the corner. I leaned for it. My hands slapped the grey pole and whipped me around. My body spun sideways. Crusher's skateboard clung to my soles. I let go at just the right time. I made the sharp turn and flew down the sidewalk. But now I was out of control. I waved my arms to keep balance. I dodged a parking meter, then a woman with a birthday cake. I ollied over a toy poodle. Thanks to the StuckTight 2000, the skateboard went where I did.

I rode an 'S' pattern between a tree, lamppost, and policeman. Maybe nothing would stop me. Maybe not. A delivery man with a hand dolly moved in front of me. I turned into the street and barely missed a speeding van. On the other side, I hopped the curb and rode into a flower garden. At that point my prayer was simple: Please, Lord, anything but roses.

When I arrived at the hospital the next day, I felt good and bad. Good, because the flowers weren't roses. Bad, because I got into a big argument with Felix over his mistake. My skateboard repair job also had me uptight. I still didn't know what Crusher thought of it. I had expected to find out at school, but he never showed up.

"He was probably so happy to get his skateboard back, he ditched school to ride it," Sam told me in the elevator.

"That sounds like something Crusher would do," I admitted. I had come to deliver more models. Some of the patients had already finished theirs and reordered. When the doors slid open I followed Sam out of the elevator. We hadn't gone far when a familiar voice sent a chill down my spine. We both stopped.

"That didn't sound like you-know-who, did it?" I asked Sam.

"Didn't I warn you?" Sam shot back.

When we were within view of the nurses' station we pressed against the wall to remain out of sight. Crusher sat in a wheelchair with a bandage around his head. White casts covered both of his wrists. His mom stood next to him filling out forms while the head nurse spoke to him.

"What happened to Crusher?" I whispered in shock.

"I don't know," Sam said in a hushed tone. "If the head nurse wasn't there, I'd go find out."

"Just go," I told her.

"Why me? You go ask him what happened, you big chicken."

"If I was a chicken, I wouldn't be in this mess," I said in my defense. "Remember the challenge I accepted? Besides, something tells me I don't want to know." I nudged Sam again. "Go on. If the head nurse sees you showing concern for a patient, you might score a few points."

"I doubt it," Sam told me. But after watching for a few more minutes, she decided to give it a try. Sam approached Crusher and the head nurse. One look at her and Crusher's face lit up, at least initially. The more he talked, the more agitated he became. I couldn't hear what he was saying, but from the spit flying and tense gestures, I could tell he wasn't a happy camper. He held up his two casts for her to see. Then he pointed at his bandaged head.

The head nurse must have told Sam to push the wheelchair, because she got behind Crusher. That's when Sam made eye contact with me. She mouthed "get lost" and jerked her head to the side. I edged back just as Crusher and his entourage headed in my direction. I slid along the wall and ducked into the first room I could find. I closed the door most of the way and stood behind it, listening. Then it occurred to me that someone was probably in the room. I turned around. I expected to see a patient glaring at me, already pushing the buzzer for the nurse.

Fortunately, God was looking out for me. I had stumbled into Mr. Meridian's room. He was asleep like the last time I came. The '59 T-Bird was displayed on the table next to his bed. He had put the red paint to good use. The body's candy apple finish looked perfect.

"He did it on purpose," Crusher's voice grumbled as he drew near. "Plummet's dead meat."

"I'm sure Willie didn't mean for you to get hurt," Sam said in my defense.

"His stupid repair job practically got me killed."

I held my breath. Crusher and company were right outside the door.

"Can I help you?" a voice from behind me asked.

I jumped, knocking the door the rest of the way closed. Mr. Meridian picked the wrong time to wake up and find me hiding. "I um ... delivered your model and ... um ..."

Mr. Meridian stared at me, giving me plenty of time for my explanation, but making it up as I went along wasn't easy. I fumbled my words, not sure what to say. Then, the voices in the hall stopped. The doorknob turned. The head nurse was probably wondering what was going on in Mr. Meridian's room.

I looked at Mr. Meridian. He nodded his head toward the closet. It was open enough for me to squeeze inside. I went for it, not sure what would happen.

A second later the head nurse knocked and burst into the room before Mr. Meridian could do anything about it. "Is everything all right in here?"

"Just fine," he told her.

There was a pause. I guessed she was trying to figure out who closed his door. I couldn't see her, but

I could hear her feet approach his bed. "I see you've made progress on the model."

"Not enough, I'm afraid." Mr. Meridian coughed.

I expected the head nurse to encourage him, but she didn't. After a period of silence, she said, "Why don't you keep the door open." Then she left.

With the head nurse back in his company, Crusher kicked into complain mode once again. He blamed his injuries on my lousy glue job. He didn't say exactly what happened, but it was obvious that he had wiped out on his skateboard thanks to my faulty repair. Since Mr. Meridian's door was still open, I remained in the closet waiting for the voices to fade. But they didn't. Sam had wheeled Crusher into the room next door to Mr. Meridian's. I could hear his bitter voice booming through the wall.

"You can come out now," Mr. Meridian said softly.

I poked my head from the closet. Mr. Meridian had sat up in bed and held the T-Bird in his hands. I ventured from my hiding place and stepped softly toward him. "Thanks for not turning me in."

He sized me up. "What are you wanted for?"

I pointed toward Crusher's room and spoke in a quiet voice. "The kid next door isn't real happy with me right now."

"I'd say not. You must be Plummet."

I nodded. "Willie Plummet. My family owns Plummet's Hobbies."

"In that case, you must be quite an expert on these things." He examined his work on the '59 T-Bird model. "I can't say this looks much like the one on the box."

"Yes it does, only better." I stepped closer to get a look myself. "How many coats of paint did you use?"

"Six. Then I rested," he said with a wink. "The Lord set the standard on that one."

"Six coats?" I marveled. I thought about how Mr. Meridian had filed down each piece in the kit. "You sure take your time. When I start a model, I want it done right away."

Mr. Meridian let out a breath and offered a faint smile. "Mr. Plummet, in my condition, nothing gets done right away. But I'm learning to accept it ... all in God's timing."

"I wish I could think that way," I said. A ray of light reflected off the '59 T-Bird. "That's one of the best paint jobs I've ever seen."

Mr. Meridian smiled and slowly turned his model to check its progress. Since finishing the paint job, he had only applied a few parts. "This is for my daughter. I want it to be just right."

"She collects model cars?"

"No. But I think she'll like this one." Mr. Meridian paused for a slow blink, as if something on his eyelids would bring a thought to mind. It did. "Can I tell you something?"

"Sure."

"When my daughter was young, my wife and I had a '59 T-Bird. She loved to go for rides with the top down. Where we went didn't matter. I used to glance in the rearview mirror and see her curls in the air. We had always planned to give her the car when she had kids of her own. It just never worked out that way."

"Why not?" I asked.

Mr. Meridian directed me to have a seat at the foot of his bed. "Eventually my wife's health failed. We had to sell the car to pay bills. Of course, my daughter understood."

I nodded, showing that I did too.

Mr. Meridian turned to look out the window. "I never stopped dreaming of buying that car for my daughter. Even after my wife died I kept praying for a way. Then I had my stroke ..." He carefully placed the model on the table. "This will have to do. I hope she understands."

I kept my eyes on the model. "I'm sure she'll love it."

Mr. Meridian took a deep breath and slowly exhaled. His eyes dropped with his shoulders.

I caught sight of the StuckTight 2000 next to the model box. After what happened to Crusher, I feared Mr. Meridian's model would crumble at any second. "So, how's the glue working out?"

"Good enough, I guess." Mr. Meridian picked up the bottle of StuckTight 2000 and looked it over. "I got some stuck on my skin that I couldn't get off, but the candy striper took care of it for me. She had some sol-vent that did the trick."

"Cool," I said. "Looks like your model is holding up okay."

Mr. Meridian handed it to me to examine. When he did, the wheel fell off. I jerked to catch it, but shook the model in the process. The bumper came loose.

"I'm sorry about that," I told him. I explained what was happening with the StuckTight 2000. "It works on some occasions and not others."

"Any idea why?"

I threw up my hands. "You got me."

"I'm sure you'll figure it out," he said, yawning. "I'm already tired again. Can you hand me that blan-ket?"

I grabbed the blanket. In the middle of the heat wave it felt weird even holding one. The hospital air conditioning was cranked high enough to freeze a polar bear. "When do you want to give the T-Bird model to your daughter?"

"She'll return from a business trip in a few days. I'd like to give it to her then."

"A few days, huh?" I glanced in the box at the hundred or so perfectly filed parts. Mr. Meridian was already dozing off. "You can do it. If you need any help, just let me know."

He pulled the covers over his shoulder. "That's mighty kind of you, Mr. Plummet. But don't give up on me yet."

"I'm not giving up on you," I said, thinking of how nice it felt to be considered kind. Now if only I could work on my patience. Tiptoeing to the door, I checked both ways. With Crusher and his attendants still in his room, this was my chance to sneak out.

An Elevator Emergency

I hurried for my next delivery, then checked in on a few patients who had tried the StuckTight 2000. I wanted to avoid them, but I had to see how the glue was working. Most felt it dried too fast and lacked holding power when it did. Some even asked me to bring them regular glue. That hurt.

Dejected, I decided to leave. Crusher's door was mostly closed. I could hear him giving orders to some-one inside. At the elevator, I pushed the down button. The doors opened to Felix standing all alone. His glasses were still stuck to his head.

"What are you doing here?" I asked.

"My dad made me come and apologize to every-one for giving the wrong story about my glasses." The elevator doors started to close, so Felix hit the open-door button.

"How has it gone?" I asked, stepping in next to him.

"Not bad so far. But I still need to see Gordy the orderly and the head nurse."

"In that case, brace yourself for the worst." I told him about Crusher and his bad attitude. "I think everyone on this floor is in a bad mood."

Just then Sam came around the corner and bolted for the elevator.

"Case in point," I said. I hit the close-door button. The stainless steel doors glided together.

"Open that!" Sam demanded. "You're not getting away that easy."

Felix reached out and hit the open-door button.

"What are you doing?" I fumed. I hit the close-door button.

"I'm getting out," he told me. He hit the open-door button.

I hit the close-door button again. Too late. Sam stepped into the elevator just as the doors closed. She quickly hit open-door.

"Willie, if my job wasn't to help people get well, I'd wring your neck," Sam sputtered, her face cinched tight.

I lifted an index finger. "Remember ... kindness. And don't forget gentleness."

"Maybe Sam's mad over what you did to Crusher," Felix reasoned. "You know, like she's sticking up for her boyfriend."

Talk about guts! Sam spun on a dime. I was glad Felix made the wisecrack and not me.

"What was that? If you actually think—" Sam stopped herself. She took a deep breath and closed her eyes. I guessed she was praying. When she spoke again, I knew she was. Sam was the model of self-control. "Felix, maybe if you cleaned your glasses you would see things more clearly."

"Can't," Felix said. "The film on my glasses is all part of my plan. It's called soap scum. That's what happens when you shower with your glasses on."

"That's disgusting," Sam said.

"Totally," I added. "Is that a chunk of soap?"

Felix crossed his eyes. "I think so. Cool, huh?"

"Cool? You mean gross!" Sam told him. "You're a health hazard. A walking germ."

"I was hoping you would say that," Felix said, feeling proud of himself. "If my mom sees it that way, she'll beg my dad to buy me new glasses."

"Give it a rest," Sam said.

"Why?" Felix protested. "Willie hasn't given up on his StuckTight 2000."

That reminded Sam of why she was so mad at me. "Thanks to your lousy glue job, I have to take care of Crusher. His wrists are broken, his ankle is sprained, and he has a concussion. He'll be here for a few days while they run some tests. Guess who gets to floss his teeth and comb his hair?"

"The luckiest candy striper on earth," I offered.

Sam was too ticked off to speak, but the steam pouring from her ears said plenty.

"Just bring him candy," Felix told her. He had learned of Crusher's sweet tooth when he sold candy at the Little League park. "Trust me. You do that and Crusher will be like putty in your hands."

"Yeah," I added. "He may even offer to floss *your* teeth."

"You think that's funny?" Sam growled. This time she hit the close-door button. When we were out of sight, Sam went for my throat. So much for self-control.

"Felix, the door!" I sputtered. "Gentleness, Sam! Gentleness!"

Felix hit the open-door button. As the steel doors parted, the head nurse came around the corner.

"Sam, what's going on in there?" she asked.

"Um, I'm checking Willie's tonsils." Sam let go of me and explained who I was.

"Oh yes, the hobby boy. We can blame you for the crutches stuck in armpits and hands stuck to wheelchairs." The head nurse glared at me, then returned her attention to Sam. "When you finish strangling him, you need to check on Leonard Grubb. He's been asking for you."

I waited for the head nurse to smile, but she didn't. She was serious on both counts. That was all Sam needed. As the doors closed, she went for my throat again. "If I have to floss Crusher's teeth and comb his hair and fluff his pillow, I'm gonna—"

"Have patience?" I suggested.

"Don't forget joy," Felix added. He jumped in between us. When that didn't work, he reached for the open-door button. Too bad his foggy glasses impaired his vision. He hit the bright red button instead—the one marked emergency.

BRINNNGGGG! the alarm wailed.

Sam let go of me. The noise was deafening. The three of us stared at the control panel on the elevator. I hit the open-door and close-door buttons, but the alarm kept ringing.

Sam finally spoke. "That does it. I'm fired."

I felt bad and wanted to reassure her, but I had a feeling she was right.

I sat sulking at the lab table. Two days had passed since my visit to Mr. Meridian. I still hadn't figured out why the StuckTight 2000 worked on some occasions and not others. The situation with Crusher was just as bad. I called to apologize, but he wouldn't talk to me. As a peace offering, I sent a new skateboard along with Sam, but he wouldn't accept it. According to Sam, all Crusher cared about was bossing her around. He expected Sam to do everything for him. The fact that he was still in the hospital was unbelievable. Sam accused him of faking his symptoms, but that made things worse. He acted even more helpless to prove that he belonged there.

The update Sam gave me on Mr. Meridian was just as depressing. The T-Bird model was still a ways from being finished. Tomorrow night his daughter would return from her business trip. Sam had taken him a regular tube of glue, but he had trouble holding the pieces in place while it dried.

I lined up all the glue bottles that I first used to make the StuckTight 2000. Felix's notes were spread out in front of me. On the one hand, I wanted to keep trying to develop the perfect formula. On the other hand, I wanted to forget the whole thing. After the elevator incident, Sam told me to stay away from the hospital. She said someone else would deliver the next order. She wouldn't tell me who it was, just someone who had planned to come by the hospital anyway.

Since Felix took the blame for sounding the emergency button, Sam didn't get in that much trouble. Her attempt to wring my neck might have even gained her a few points with the head nurse. Felix got off almost as easy as Sam did, probably because his dad had served as the engineer for the hospital's construction.

The Axle Avenger was still parked on the end of the lab table. The parts filled a cardboard box next to it. I grabbed the remote and hit the forward lever. The Axle Avenger didn't move. Before last night, I was set to rebuild. With the bonding power of the StuckTight 2000, my car would destroy any car in its path. Or so I had thought. Then reality hit. First, Crusher's skateboard broke in two. Then, the parts on Mr. Meridian's T-Bird model fell off.

I picked up the Axle Avenger. Seeing it reminded me of Mr. Meridian's T-Bird. I felt guilty just thinking about what started my quest for the perfect glue—impatience. I could have waited for the glue to dry, but I had to race. What a contrast to Mr. Meridian. His hands weren't listening to his head. His daughter was due to return soon. If anyone needed a glue that bonded on contact and held like steel, it was him. Yet he waited patiently to apply each part. He did the best he could, completely at peace.

I was the exact opposite, which didn't make sense. I knew that believing in Jesus as Lord and Savior meant I had His forgiveness and eternal life. But it also meant I received the fruits of His Spirit. The Spirit produced joy, patience, kindness, and all kinds of godly qualities—qualities I saw in Mr. Meridian.

I prayed while walking around the lab, asking God to forgive me for my bad attitude. Soon, I had a new motivation for developing the perfect glue. I could improve the StuckTight 2000 for someone other than myself. "That's it," I blurted out. "Mr. Meridian, this glue's for you."

"Willie, who are you talking to?" Amanda asked. She stood in the doorway that led from the lab to the front of the store. "Sorry to interrupt you and your imaginary friend, but there's an actual person here to see you."

Megan stepped past Amanda into the lab. "Hi, Willie."

"Oh, hi, Megan," I said, standing up. I straightened my hair with my fingers. "What's going on?"

"Not much," Megan offered with a smile. "I just came by to get an order. Sam told me she called it in."

"Um ... yeah." I leaned an elbow on the lab table, but that felt awkward, like I was trying to pose for a picture. I stood and crossed my arms. "The models are behind the register."

Megan shrugged. "Okay. Thanks."

I rolled on my feet, going from heel to toe. "Sure. No problem."

Amanda just stood there staring at us, grinning from ear to ear. "This is cute."

"What?" I asked, glaring at my sister.

"Nothing." Amanda copied me by rolling from heel to toe. "No problem."

My face burned. Megan was probably wondering what my sister was implying. And so was I. The silence felt heavy, so I cleared my throat in Amanda's direction. She gave me a wink, then left.

"So, you're the new delivery service, huh?" I asked. This time I leaned a stiff arm on the table. My triceps flexed beneath my shirt. I hoped Megan noticed.

"Yeah. I was going to visit Sam anyway to find out about being a candy striper. This gave me a reason to make it today." Megan looked around, ending with the table. "Are you rebuilding your model?"

"Not yet. First, I want to invent a glue that will hold it together. So far, I've struck out." I told her about the StuckTight 2000 and the problems it caused, finishing with Mr. Meridian. "I don't understand it. The StuckTight 2000 worked great at first; not just in the lab, but on Crusher's skateboard too."

Megan admitted to hearing some of Mr. Meridian's story from Sam. "I wish I could help, but I don't know anything about glue."

"That makes two of us," I joked.

We stared at the glues. Megan broke the awkward silence with a sigh. "Whew. At least you have a cool place to work. It's like an oven outside."

"You should have been in here a few days ago. It was hot, real hot. We just got the air conditioner fixed today." I looked back at the lab table. The wheels in my head started to turn. "Wait a minute!"

"What?" Megan asked.

I grabbed a bottle of StuckTight 2000. I put a drop on a plastic toothpick. It dried in seconds. Time for the test. I pushed at the toothpick. It went right over. "That's it! When the glue is warm, it holds. When it cools down, it breaks! Megan, you're the best."

She looked bewildered. "Thanks ... I guess."

I explained my theory. "Crusher used his skateboard in the morning when it was still cold outside. The hospital is cold too. But when we made the StuckTight 2000 and first tested it, the temperature was hot. Our air conditioner was broken. The glue bonds on skin, because skin is warm."

"Sounds like you have it figured out. Now what?"

"Modify." I squeezed some of the StuckTight 2000 into a large plastic bottle. Next, I grabbed the glue marked number seven and put in several drops. "This one claims to have the most strength of any glue."

"What about that one?" Megan asked, pointing to a plastic cement.

"Number nine?" I checked the label. "It says, 'Keep away from children.' You better stand back."

Megan didn't so much as grin. "Real funny."

I swallowed what felt like my tongue. I couldn't believe I had tried Felix's lame line on Megan. "Um ... anyway ... it supposedly dries fast. Let's try it." I squeezed the tube until the clear goop oozed into the mixing bottle.

Next, I had a suggestion of my own. Then Megan had another. Pretty soon we were mixing glues, epoxies, and cements like nobody's business. We added one sample after another. When glue got on our hands, we wiped it off and kept mixing until the bottle was full. I finished with several drops of drying catalyst.

"That ought to do the trick," I said, trying to sound confident. I had a nagging feeling I was forgetting something. With Megan standing next to me, I couldn't think straight.

"Now what?" Megan asked.

"We test it." I put a drop on the Axle Avenger's antenna and held it in place on the hood.

"Is it holding?" Megan asked.

"I think so." I let go and watched. The antenna held its position. I gave it a nudge. It held like steel. "Yes! We did it! High five!" I brought my right hand up and Megan slapped it with her left. We squeezed hard to celebrate our accomplishment.

"All right!" Megan cheered. "Let's hear it for the Stuck-Tight 2000!"

As we lowered our hands, I felt her grip loosen. Mine did too. But for some reason our hands didn't come apart. Our eyes met for a moment, then we looked away. I tried to swallow, but my mouth was desert dry. Thanks to the glue, we were holding hands.

"Um ... I think our hands are stuck together," I finally mumbled.

"I don't mind," Megan said with a smile.

That threw me. I didn't know if my heart would go into overdrive or stop completely. My eyes darted around the lab, as if what I should say would be on a cue card somewhere. It wasn't. I fumbled for the right words—any words.

Before they came, Amanda entered the lab from the front of the store. "Willie, Dad needs you to straighten the models in the boat aisle."

"Um ... sure. Tell him I'll be there soon," I said weakly, fearful my voice would crack.

"Are you all right?" Amanda asked. She came around the table.

"Yeah, fine," I told her. I pushed closer to Megan and hid our hands beneath the table.

"Me too," Megan said. "I'm fine."

"See," I shrugged. "I'm fine. She's fine. We're both fine. Fine. Fine."

Amanda's eyes shifted between me and Megan. She glanced down at the table. Her dopey grin returned, followed by a wink. "I'll tell Dad you'll be out soon, and that you're both fine. Fine. Fine."

Megan waited for Amanda to leave before talking. "Why didn't you just tell her about our hands getting glued together?"

"Are you crazy? You should have heard her when my pillow got glued to my face. This is worse, way worse."

"Worse? What makes this so much worse?" Megan's eyes narrowed as she moved away from me.

"Um ... I didn't mean it like that," I fumbled. "Holding your hand is—"

"Willie," Orville spouted off, barging into the lab. "Dad wants to know how long you'll be?"

"As I told Amanda, *soon.*" Squeezing next to Megan, I moved our hands under the table again.

Orville looked us over, then meandered around the lab.

"What are you looking for?" I asked.

"Oh, nothing." Orville dropped to his knees to check some lower shelves along the back wall. Before standing, he glanced quickly in our direction.

I was ready for him. In the instant his head turned toward us, I raised our hands so that they were above the table. When Orville stood up, I lowered them again. He finally took the hint and left, looking like he was trying to keep from laughing.

It was time to straighten things out with Megan. "When I said worse, I meant they would tease me worse. That's all."

Megan smiled. "So what do we do about this?"

"Oh, yeah. My dad's Super Solvent will take this off. It's over there." I used my free hand to point to the shelf.

Leaving the protection of the table wasn't easy. I stepped around the end of it and Megan followed. We were halfway to the shelf when my mom barged in the back door of the lab.

"You can't believe what song they're playing," she announced. My mom hurried to the radio on the back shelf and turned it on. She found the right station and cranked it up. "It came on just as I parked."

"Stuck on you," the singer crooned. "Got this feeling down deep in my soul that I just can't lose ..." The guy sounded like a lovesick puppy.

My mom hummed along, then called to the front of the store. "Honey, come back here. Bring Orville and Amanda."

The three of them rushed into the lab.

"What is it?" my dad asked.

"It's Lionel," my mom told him.

"Mom, Lionel makes trains," Orville pointed out.

"Not this Lionel," Mom replied. "This is Lionel Richie. He's singing 'Stuck On You,' the song I told you about the other day. Couldn't you just die?"

"I know I could," I mumbled.

That's when my mom noticed Megan and the fact that our hands were together. "I'm sorry, Willie. I didn't know you had company."

I introduced Megan. She and my mom exchanged greetings while I stood there melting.

Amanda and Orville hummed along with the tune while watching me and Megan. They grinned like monkeys. Mom and Dad did the same.

"Yep. That's Lionel Richie," my dad admitted. "I remember this now."

"See," my mom replied. She sang along. " 'Well, I'm on my way ...' "

My dad joined her. " 'Mighty glad you stayed.' "

Before long, Orville and Amanda tried to sing along too. They didn't like '80s music or even know the words, but that didn't stop them. They faked it for my sake. Witnessing the most embarrassing moment of my life was too good to pass up.

I thought the song would never end. When it did, my mom spoke up first. "Well, I guess we should mind the store."

"Yep," Orville agreed. "Mind the store."

"What about the store?" Amanda asked, still watching me and Megan.

"Whose store?" my dad wanted to know. He eyed Megan's hand in mine, then gave me a nod. *That's my boy*, was written all over his face.

"Our store," Mom answered. "Better get out there."

They did, finally. Megan and I strolled to the back shelf and grabbed the bottle of Super Solvent.

"Well, I guess we should open it," Megan said.

"Yeah, I guess so."

I held the bottle while Megan turned the lid. The Super Solvent felt cool as it seeped between our palms and fingers. As much as I wanted to be free, part of me wanted to stall a little longer. Having my hand stuck to Megan's wasn't so bad after all.

The next day I found Megan on the front steps of our school. We had a few minutes until class started, so I sat down beside her. The awkwardness from yesterday returned.

"So how'd the delivery go?" I asked.

She glanced at me, then looked away. "Fine. Mr. Meridian seemed glad to get the improved StuckTight 2000 and the Super Solvent."

"How's the '59 T-Bird coming along?" I asked.

Before Megan could answer, Sam and Mitch joined us. "One more day of Crusher and I quit. I can't take it anymore."

"Did it get worse after I left?" Megan asked.

"Way worse. Last night I had to floss Crusher's teeth. That was *after* he spent the day chewing beef jerky."

Mitch grabbed Sam's hand and started counting her fingers. "At least you still have ten left."

"But for how long?" Sam pulled her hand away and made a fist. "I want him out, now!"

"Patience, patience," Felix said, coming over. He tried to sit down between me and Megan, but there wasn't room.

"Watch it!" I told him.

"Sorry," Felix said. Rather than move, he sat down anyway, forcing us to slide apart.

I started to get mad, then noticed his glasses. No wonder he misjudged how much room there was. His glasses were filthy, like an old bottle you would find at the dump.

"Felix, your glasses are beyond gross," Sam said. "As an official hospital candy striper, I can't let you wear those anymore. The Surgeon General would declare them hazardous to your health."

"My mom feels the same way. She thinks I've suffered enough," Felix said with a smile. "My dad agrees. He told me to get these off and clean them up. If I can take care of them for one more day, I get new glasses. I told him I'd stop by the lab after school for some Super Solvent."

I shook my head. "Sorry. I sent the last of it with Megan to the hospital, along with the new improved bottle of StuckTight 2000."

"So we'll go to the hospital," Felix said.

"No you won't," Sam put in. "The head nurse will go ballistic if she catches either of you on her floor. Thanks to Crusher, she's really on edge."

"We can stay out of sight," I reasoned. "Besides, I want to check in on Mr. Meridian. I'll bet his model T-Bird is almost done."

Sam's eyes dimmed. She glanced at Megan, but not at me.

"What's wrong?" I asked. "Didn't the StuckTight 2000 help?"

Sam answered. "Mr. Meridian used it for a little while, then he let someone else borrow it. He was really tired and unsteady."

I looked at Megan, then Sam. "What do you mean?"

"He's not doing very well," Sam said. "With his daughter coming tonight, I don't think he will finish on time even with the improved StuckTight 2000."

"In that case, I have to visit him this afternoon," I said. "Come on, Sam. What do you think?"

The bell rang before Sam could answer. She stood up along with the rest of us.

"Well?" I asked.

Sam crossed her arms, mulling it over. "Just don't tell the head nurse you're with me, 'cause you're not. And bring more StuckTight 2000. It was going fast."

"More glue, huh?" I asked. My eyes met Megan's. "I can't. I sort of forgot to take notes."

"What?" Felix gagged. "After all we went through? What were you thinking?"

"It's my fault," Megan said. "I was helping and got in the way."

Felix looked at us both. "Am I missing something here?"

"It's your glasses," I said. "You can't expect to see everything."

"That's not what I meant."

I tried to remember what Megan and I had used to improve the StuckTight 2000. I could picture some of the bottles and tubes, but not all of them. "What a drag. First, Mr. Meridian had to settle for a model to give his daughter instead of the real '59 T-Bird, and now he won't even finish that."

"Speaking of the T-Bird, there it is!" Felix jerked his hand toward the street. But thanks to his blurry glasses, he poked Mitch in the eye.

"Ouch!" Mitch cringed. He bent over, covering his eye.

We gathered around him.

"Are you all right?" Sam asked.

Mitch removed his hand. His eye was still closed. "I don't know. Felix pushed my eyeball halfway to my brain."

"Sorry," Felix said. "But there's the T-Bird that almost hit me!" He pointed again and we all ducked. Then we followed his hand to the street.

"That's a VW Rabbit!" I told him.

"Are you sure?" Felix asked.

"He's sure," Sam added, heading for class. "Remember what I said. When you come to the hospital, *neither* of you is with me."

When we arrived at the hospital, Felix and I moved like undercover spies.

"I still can't believe you held Megan's hand in the lab," Felix said.

"I can't believe you nearly poked Mitch's eye out," I replied.

We pressed our backs against the wall and glanced around the corner. The elevator was open, so we went for it. Felix didn't want the vice president, or any of the other administrators, to see his dirty glasses.

We breathed a little easier when the stainless steel doors slid shut. When the doors opened on the third floor, we panicked again, not sure who would be waiting for us. Fortunately, the lobby was empty. After what Sam said, I didn't want to bump into the head nurse. Avoiding Crusher was also on the top of my list.

Felix followed me past the nurses' station and down the corridor to the physical rehab unit. Everything was going great until he bumped into a cart with cleaning supplies. He hit it so hard it flew into my ankle. I stumbled before regaining my balance.

"You're dangerous," I told him, certain the head nurse would appear. "First Mitch, now me."

"Look who's talking. Thanks to you, Crusher is still in the hospital."

I limped ahead, feeling conspicuous. Felix followed. We were almost to Mr. Meridian's room when a voice caught our attention.

"Psst!" Sam whispered.

She came out of a room behind us and motioned for us to follow. She stopped in front of a small storage room and handed me the bottle of Super Solvent. "Conserve it. There's not much left."

"What about the StuckTight 2000?" I asked.

"I put it in Mr. Meridian's room. It's almost gone too." A bell caught Sam's attention. "Not again."

"What?" Felix asked.

"That's Crusher. He probably wants me to trim his toenails or something."

I made a face like I would throw up.

"Kindness, Sam," Felix urged. "Kindness."

In the storage room, I found a cotton ball and dabbed it with Super Solvent. Felix held both sides of his glasses. "Ouch. It burns a little. Is it supposed to?"

"I think it's because of the rash from the glue. Either that or your nose will fall off."

"Real funny," Felix said.

"Haven't you seen those glasses with the nose attached? Now you know why they have them."

"Real funny again." Felix closed his eyes and said a short prayer. "Here it goes." He pulled at the frames. The skin held tight.

"Harder," I said.

Felix gritted his teeth and tugged. The bond against his skin came loose, but so did the bond that held the glasses together. Each hand held half of the frames. Felix looked like he would cry. "So close. Only one day. One more day."

I patted his back. "Just tape them together. Your dad will understand."

"No, he won't. So much for new glasses. I'll be the pencil-splint kid for life."

"Tape them," I told him. "Just do it. I'm going to check on Mr. Meridian." I felt bad leaving Felix in the storage room like that. I'd send Sam back to help him.

Mr. Meridian was asleep. The model of the T-Bird was on a table next to his bed. Sam was right about its condition. It was only half done. The bumper was crooked. The windshield had glue smudges on it. The engine was in pieces next to the bright red body. I checked my watch. Mr. Meridian's daughter was due to arrive in a couple of hours. I listened to Mr. Meridian snore and considered waking him. But I knew not to; he needed his rest.

Then I thought of something better, way better. I would finish the '59 T-Bird for him. Mr. Meridian would wake up and there it would be. His daughter would get her gift after all.

Stepping to the table, I picked up the bottle of StuckTight 2000. It was almost gone. I'd have to use it sparingly. I put it down and picked up the Super Solvent. I removed the crooked parts and cleaned the windshield.

That's when Mr. Meridian stirred. I ducked beneath the table. He grumbled and smacked his gums. I held my breath and prayed, not knowing what to do if he woke up. Mr. Meridian muttered to himself, tugged at his sheets, then rolled over. Before long he was snoring again.

I grabbed the bottle of StuckTight 2000 and started gluing the T-Bird together. I put the seats in place, then the floor mats. Next, I worked on the speedometer and doors. I attached the headlights. It only took a drop of StuckTight 2000 to do the trick. With each part, the T-Bird looked better and better. *I can do this*, I thought. Then I glanced in the box and reality hit. More than fifty parts remained. StuckTight 2000 or not, it would take a miracle to finish the T-Bird before Mr. Meridian's daughter arrived.

I dropped my head in sorrow and closed my eyes to pray. Too many parts and only one of me. I'd never make it. I had failed at patience. I had failed at self-control. Now when I tried to offer a simple act of kindness, I had failed again. I felt miserable. Other people could practice spiritual fruit in their lives, why couldn't I?

My head was still bowed when the Lord gave me an answer. It just took me a little while to figure it out.

Team StuckTight

A familiar voice in the hall caught my attention, followed by footsteps, lots of them.

"This way," Sam said in a hushed tone. Suddenly, she appeared in the doorway, along with Felix, Mitch, and Megan.

I put my finger over my lips, then met them in the hall. Mitch had a patch over his eye.

"Was it that bad?" I whispered to him.

Mitch shook his head. "It was still bothering me, so Sam fixed me up."

"Me too," Felix said. He pointed to the white tape holding his glasses together.

Sam glanced in Mr. Meridian's room and noticed the model. "He'll never finish it in time, will he?"

"Nope." I told them how I had wanted to finish it for him. "There's just too much to do."

Without a word, Megan tiptoed into Mr. Meridian's room. The rest of us followed. She looked in the

box, then back at the T-Bird. Her face spelled doubt.
She wasn't alone. But when I looked at Mr. Meridian
sleeping peacefully, I decided I wouldn't give up.
Years ago he had given up on giving the real T-Bird to
his daughter. Now all he hoped for was a toy replica,
and his trembling and tired hands wouldn't even
allow that.

But mine would. Maybe I wouldn't finish in time,
but if I failed, it wouldn't be because I failed to try.
"There's enough StuckTight 2000 left to finish it. If we
all help, we can do it."

Megan spoke first. "I'll go for it."

That made the difference. Mitch gave me the
thumbs up.

Felix started to nod, but stopped himself when
his glasses slid to the end of his nose. "I'll give it a
shot. Just save the last drop of StuckTight 2000 for my
glasses."

"Deal," I said.

Sam watched the hall while she whispered. "I'll
help as much as I can. It all depends on how much the
head nurse needs me ... and Crusher."

"Then what are we waiting for?" Megan asked.
She moved beside me and grabbed two parts. Mitch
followed.

Everyone grabbed pieces and got to work. It felt
like we were on the assembly line for Ford. Sam held
up parts. Megan applied the glue. Felix, Mitch, and I
assembled.

Ding, ding! Crusher's bell rang.

We held our breath and watched Mr. Meridian. He stirred but kept snoring.

"What now?" Sam muttered. She hurried next door to Crusher's room.

She returned ten minutes later, her eyes fierce. She mimicked what she had just endured. "'Sam, fluff my pillow. Sam, brush my teeth. Sam, my hair's a mess.' If he rings that bell again, his hair won't be the only thing that's a mess."

Mitch pressed his lips together to keep from laughing. It didn't work. He let out a snicker.

That's what Sam needed to see. She laughed in spite of herself. "I'm sorry, you guys. I'm trying to be patient with Crusher. I pray about my attitude all the time. But he's pushing me to the edge."

"After all you've put up with, you deserve an award," Megan said softly. "Like candy striper of the year."

As we whispered, we continued to work. Pretty soon, the T-Bird took on a new look. We were grateful, especially considering our circumstances. I felt kind of nervous around Megan, and I think she felt the same. Felix's glasses kept sliding down his nose. Mitch had a sore eye. And Sam had to keep leaving to help Crusher. Through it all, Mr. Meridian's snoring gave us permission to continue. In a strange sort of way, the sound was even comforting.

We were nearly done when Mr. Meridian muttered the loudest. I made a down motion with my hands. Everyone dropped below the surface of the table and huddled together.

That was a mistake. Big time.

When Mr. Meridian's snoring kicked in again, we stood up. But we didn't split up. The StuckTight 2000 on our fingers had bonded us together. Mitch's hand was stuck to Sam's back. My hand was glued to Felix's shoulder. Felix's fingers were glued to Megan's arm. And Megan had a hand stuck to Sam's waist.

"Why me?" Sam whimpered. "Why me?"

Felix used his free hand to reach for the bottle of Super Solvent. But he quickly found out what I already knew. It was gone. All of it, gone. To make things worse, Crusher rang.

Our eyes darted to Sam. She just shook her head. "If he wants to get me fired, fine. I've tried to be patient and kind. I've prayed about it. What else can I do?"

Crusher rang away.

Mr. Meridian stopped snoring. We all huddled down again, hoping Crusher would stop before Mr. Meridian woke up. Too bad Crusher didn't and Mr. Meridian did.

"Hold your horses," Mr. Meridian said, his voice groggy. "She'll get there as soon as she can."

Crusher ignored him. When Mr. Meridian said something else, Crusher shouted back. "Mind your own business!"

Soon we heard the heavy heels of the head nurse clopping into Crusher's room. They argued for a few minutes, then the head nurse left. Minutes later, Gordy the orderly went past Mr. Meridian's room pushing a wheelchair. We heard more complaining next door, followed by Crusher leaving his room in a wheelchair pushed by Gordy. That explained it. Crusher liked Sam to take him around the grounds at sunset. The head nurse was probably just as mad as Crusher that Sam couldn't be found and reluctantly had sent Gordy instead.

Sam stared at the floor. She probably thought that she was finished at the hospital. I would have consoled her, but with Mr. Meridian awake, speaking was out of the question. Finishing his model would be too, if he didn't fall asleep soon.

After tossing and turning for a few minutes, Mr. Meridian closed his eyes. Minutes later, the snoring returned.

"Now what?" Megan asked.

Before I could answer, Sam did for me. "We finish what we started. I told Crusher I was busy with something and not to ring me. If he got me fired, that's his problem. Helping Mr. Meridian was the right thing to do."

That was just what we needed to hear. Except Mitch, we all had one free hand. I picked up a hub cap and Megan held the bottle of glue. Felix and Sam attached a bumper. The engine came next. I lowered it in place while the others held the frame. Little by little we glued parts until we were down to the antenna.

But when I held it out for glue, none came. Megan squeezed the bottle. We all stared at the tip, waiting for just a drop. Nothing. She shook the bottle. Then Sam hit the end while Megan held it. Finally, a tiny drop appeared, that was all. I touched the antenna to it and put it in place. "Down to the last drop," I said.

We put the model on the table and stood back to check it out. It looked perfect. Everyone was beaming. Everyone except Felix.

"The last drop," he said. Using my shoulder, he pushed his glasses back up. "Oh well, it was worth it. I'll just tell my dad what happened. At least we helped Mr. Meridian."

Sam gave Felix a nod. "I couldn't have said it better myself."

We started for the door when we heard voices coming down the hall.

"That's the head nurse," Sam whispered.

"She's with someone," Felix said. "It sounds like a woman."

"I'll bet it's Mr. Meridian's daughter." I started for the door, but didn't get far, not with my hand glued to Felix. "Hurry up."

Sam held us back. "We'll never make it."

"Let's hide," Mitch suggested.

I edged toward the closet. Everyone followed. We moved like a giant amoeba. We took little steps. I never thought we'd fit, but somehow we managed to squeeze together and close the door just in time.

"Dad, time to wake up," a woman's voice sang.

"Huh? What?" Mr. Meridian asked. We heard sheets rustle as he sat up in bed. A peck on the cheek followed. "How's my girl?"

"Great," she said. After a pause, she spoke again. "What's this?"

"That's just something I—" Mr. Meridian stopped mid-sentence. I was sure he had just discovered the completed '59 T-Bird. "Well, I'll be ... all in God's timing."

"It's beautiful, Dad," she told him.

I felt Felix tap me. One look and I knew why. His glasses had slid all the way down his nose. Before any of us could stop them, they fell. I raised my foot to cushion their fall. It worked, but then I couldn't put my foot down. What if I stepped on them? I tried to keep my balance, but started to wobble. From there, it was all over.

The sound was loud. I fell into the sliding door. Everyone came with me. The door popped out of its tracks, and we all fell into the room.

A Sunset Cruise

We must have looked like a human glueball when we tumbled to the floor.

The head nurse went ballistic. "Samantha Stewart, what on earth are you doing?"

Sam fumbled through an explanation, but Mr. Meridian cut her off.

"So you're the ones I should thank," Mr. Meridian said. He nodded at the model, then spoke to his daughter. "I started the T-Bird, but I needed a little help from my friends to finish it."

"Your friends, huh?" the head nurse said. "Looks like they had a little glue trouble."

"Glasses, too," Felix added. He retrieved his glasses. As soon as he put them on, they fell apart. The head nurse picked up one half. Sam grabbed the other. They tried to put them back together, but it was no use.

"That's okay," Felix said. "Don't worry about it."

I felt bad for Felix and proud of him at the same time. I knew how much getting new glasses meant to him. But he put off what he wanted to help Mr. Meridian. He knew it was worth it. We all did.

Mr. Meridian sat up in bed as his daughter brought the '59 T-Bird over from the table. They pointed out each detail, remembering their car from so many years ago.

"What a wonderful surprise, Daddy," his daughter said. "Now I have one for you. But you have to come outside to see it."

Mr. Meridian grinned. "I'm feeling better after my rest. Let's go."

His daughter nodded at the wheelchair in the corner of the room. "Have your friends bring you down. I'll meet you in the front."

"But we're stuck together," I protested.

"Not your feet," the head nurse chimed in. "I'll even hold the elevator door for you."

We waited in the hall while Mr. Meridian changed his clothes. When he came out, he had on a derby hat and tweed coat. He sat tall in the wheelchair. "Ready when you are."

Felix grabbed one handle and Megan and I grabbed the other. We must have looked ridiculous pushing him along. But that didn't stop us. We kept going, feeling fine. We were halfway down the hall when Gordy the orderly appeared with Crusher at the other end.

"Finally!" Crusher shouted. "You're mine, Plummet. So are you, Stewart."

Gordy picked up the pace in our direction.

"Are you thinking what I'm thinking?" I whispered to Felix.

"Bingo," he said.

We explained our plan to Mr. Meridian. He liked it. No, that's not true. He loved it.

"Up for a little game of chicken, young man?" Mr. Meridian called out.

"Yeah, right," Crusher scoffed.

We increased our speed. So did Gordy. Without his glasses, Felix had a tough time of it. He stepped on my shoe and gave me a flat. "Sorry," he told me.

"No problem, Felix. Just keep moving."

He did. And so did Gordy. The gap closed to thirty feet, then twenty. Mr. Meridian clenched the armrest on the wheelchair.

Ten feet. Five.

"No!" Crusher wailed.

We held our course.

Crusher squirmed. "You're crazy!"

Three feet. Two. One.

"Turn away! Turn!" Crusher shouted. He curled into a ball and winced.

Gordy turned just in time.

"All right!" Mr. Meridian cheered. The rest of us did too.

As we kept our course for the elevator and Crusher faded in the distance, we could still hear him complaining to Gordy.

Gordy just kept repeating, "You told me to turn. You told me."

We caught the elevator and all headed into the main lobby. The vice president was waiting for us ... along with Felix's dad.

Felix explained what happened to his glasses. "I'm sorry, Dad. I tried not to break them. I promise. Then we ran out of glue."

"You really tried?" Mr. Patterson asked.

Everyone nodded.

Mr. Patterson looked at the vice president, then back at Felix. "When you're finished here, meet us in the optometry department."

"You got it!" Felix let out.

We celebrated with him, then resumed our walk. We pushed through the front doors. Mr. Meridian's wheelchair led the way.

"What's going on here?" Mr. Meridian asked, searching for his daughter. A moment later his question was answered. His daughter pulled up in a 1959 red T-Bird. It looked brand new, like she had brought it straight from the showroom floor.

"Going my way?" his daughter asked.

Mr. Meridian's mouth dropped open. "Is that our car?"

"Sure is," his daughter said. "It took me years to find it, but last week it all came together."

Suddenly, his daughter's face looked familiar. "You're the one who sped through the neighborhood," I said. "But that car was black."

She explained that she had just picked up the T-Bird that morning and was still learning to handle it. The original color had been painted over, so she left it in the shop while she was away on business. The guy we saw driving it up the hill must have been the mechanic. "Well, what do you think, Dad?"

"I love it."

"I hope so," his daughter said. "It's yours."

"Mine? But I wanted you to have this car," Mr. Meridian sighed, still managing a smile. "Besides, I'm afraid my driving days are over."

"In that case, I'll be your chauffeur," his daughter replied. She helped him into the front seat and everyone gathered around. At least twenty people were on hand. Even the head nurse appeared. She held a brown bottle.

"What's that?" Sam asked.

"I called Plummet's Hobbies. Mr. Plummet gave me the ingredients for his Super Solvent. We had the chemicals on hand, so I had Gordy mix up a batch." She soaked a cotton ball with Super Solvent and dabbed it on our glued areas. Soon we were free.

"Who wants to join us for a spin?" Mr. Meridian asked. "The back seat is wide open."

"I'd love to," Felix said, "but I have an appointment in the optometry department."

The head nurse spoke up next. "I don't know what you kids did to Crusher, but he's quiet as a mouse." Then she turned to Sam. "Normally, I'd ask for an explanation, but after all you've put up with, I don't need one. You've proven yourself to me."

"You mean I'm not fired?" Sam asked.

"Fired? Of course not. You're an excellent candy striper—the model of patience."

"Awesome," Sam said. She gave the head nurse a hug. The Spirit had been working through Sam all along; she was just too hard on herself to realize it.

"And don't worry about Crusher," the head nurse went on. "We're moving him into Mr. Higgins' room tonight. I don't think he will be faking it much longer."

"Thank you," Sam said. She pretended to wipe the sweat from her forehead. Then she brought up Mitch's eye injury. The head nurse agreed to have a look at it. The three of them headed inside. That left me and Megan standing on the curb.

"Well, what are you two waiting for?" Mr. Meridian asked.

I turned to Megan. "Are you up for a ride?"

"Ready when you are."

We climbed in the back. As the T-Bird started off, we felt the cool breeze in our faces. The heat wave had finally broken. Patience, I thought to myself. Patience. Nothing worked out as soon as I thought it would. But eventually, in God's timing, things do work out.

I decided that my glue inventing days were through. A glue that bonds on contact and holds like steel is more trouble than it's worth. Someday I would rebuild the Axle Avenger, but I would use regular plastic cement. I would be patient and do it right.

But that would come later. Right then I was right where I wanted to be: in a classic car, cruising with the top down. The sunset filled the sky with color. When the radio came on, I couldn't believe my ears. The song playing was "Stuck on You." Megan noticed and we started to laugh. We even exchanged a high five. Squeezing tight, we left our hands together just like before. But this time it had nothing to do with glue.

Look for all these
exciting
WiLLiE PLuMMeT
misadventures
at your local
Christian
bookstore!